TORMENTED LOVE

GW00362351

Shangri-La—a deceptively beautiful
name for the house Amie had been
left in Mauritius by her unknown
uncle. For the house was all he *had* left
her; all his money had gone to Oliver
Maxwell. It wasn't difficult to con-
clude that her uncle had hoped that
that she and Oliver would settle the
question by marrying each other—
but how could she marry a maddening
man like that, who didn't care a fig for
her anyway?

Books you will enjoy
by MARGARET MAYO

A TASTE OF PARADISE

An island in the Indian Ocean for a wedding present! As if marrying her boss wasn't excitement enough, Cathy thought, as she travelled happily out to inspect the place. But she arrived to find that the situation was not quite as her fiancé had told her it was, and there were problems. Notably the unyielding Grant Howard!

INNOCENT BRIDE

Jonita couldn't have been in a worse predicament—stranded in Portugal, with no job and not even the fare home. She should have been grateful to Druce Devereux when he came up with a solution to her problem—but she suspected it would only lead her into worse trouble. And how right she was!

PIRATE LOVER

Just about everything had gone wrong with Tammy's holiday in the South of France, and when she lost her handbag and all her luggage into the bargain she reckoned she had reached rock bottom. But no—for next she found herself crossing swords with Hugo Kane, who not only looked like a pirate but behaved like one as well!

VALLEY OF THE HAWK

When Corrie discovered that her real mother was living in Ireland, she couldn't resist going off to look for her. She didn't find her—but instead she met Damon Courtney, who jumped to all the wrong conclusions about her—and turned her life upside down in the process!

TORMENTED LOVE

BY

MARGARET MAYO

MILLS & BOON LIMITED
15-16 BROOK'S MEWS
LONDON W1A 1DR

All the characters in this book have no existence outside the imagination of the Author, and have no relation whatsoever to anyone bearing the same name or names. They are not even distantly inspired by any individual known or unknown to the Author, and all the incidents are pure invention.

The text of this publication or any part thereof may not be reproduced or transmitted in any form or by any means, electronic or mechanical, including photocopying, recording, storage in an information retrieval system, or otherwise, without the written permission of the publisher.

This book is sold subject to the condition that it shall not, by way of trade or otherwise, be lent, resold, hired out or otherwise circulated without the prior consent of the publisher in any form of binding or cover other than that in which it is published and without a similar condition being imposed on the subsequent purchaser.

First published 1980
Australian copyright 1981
Philippine copyright 1981
This edition 1981

© Margaret Mayo 1980

ISBN 0 263 73512 5

Set in Linotype Baskerville 11 on 12 pt.

Made and printed in Great Britain by
Richard Clay (The Chaucer Press), Ltd., Bungay, Suffolk

CHAPTER ONE

AFTER the accident the news that she had inherited her uncle's house should have cheered Amie Douglas; instead she received the information with no more enthusiasm than if she had won five pounds in a prize draw.

She re-read the letter dispassionately, then finished her breakfast and automatically began to clear the table. Even this simple task took so much longer and tears sprang to her eyes as yet another cup fell to the floor.

Staring down at the smashed pieces, she reflected that this was what had happened to her life. In a matter of minutes her career, her whole future, had been ruined, broken into a thousand tiny fragments.

No one could begin to guess at the despair she felt each time she tried to pick up something only to find it slipping from her nerveless fingers. Her only consolation was that at least she was still alive. Poor Ginny had not made it; the accident had proved the end of the road for her.

Reliving those terrifying moments, Amie could hear again Ginny's scream when the car went out of control. She closed her eyes, clapping her hands to her ears as if to try and shut out the blood-curdling sound.

It had been a good party, but her friend had drunk too much and Amie had insisted on driving. Black ice made the roads treacherous and she had driven with extra care, but when a dog ran out in front of them she had instinctively braked. The car had swung out of control and hit a tree. Poor Ginny had never recovered consciousness.

It had been Amie's idea to go to the party, given by one of her student friends, and now she blamed herself. If they hadn't gone none of this would have happened. Ginny would still be here sharing her flat and Amie would be continuing her course at the college.

She had set her mind on a fashion career, designing clothes, fabrics, anything connected with the world of fashion. Now it was over. The thoughts were there but she had no way of carrying them out. Trying to use her left hand was farcical; the spidery shapes that covered the paper on her first attempt made her give up without even trying again.

It was bad enough making up her face and doing simple everyday tasks with one hand, but trying to hold a pencil and make it go where she wanted was impossible. She managed to write, a thin spidery script that looked nothing like her normal bold outlines, but actual designing was out of the question.

Her right arm had been crushed, a livid scar told its own story. The doctors assured her that it would fade in time and that plastic surgery was not out of the question if it bothered her greatly. But plastic surgery wouldn't give her back the use of her fingers!

This lack of feeling puzzled the doctors. There was no reason, they said, why she should not be able to use her hand, but she couldn't, no matter how she tried. They said it was purely psychological, she was blaming herself for Ginny's death, punishing herself in the way that mattered most. They suggested physiotherapy.

Amie didn't believe them and refused. No one but an idiot would will themselves not to be able to use their right hand when it meant everything to them. The doctors were out of their minds.

She picked up the broken pieces one by one and dropped them into the kitchen bin, then she finished clearing the table and washed up, leaving the dishes to dry in the rack. She made her bed and tidied the flat and then when there was nothing else left to do she picked up her father's letter and read again the astounding news that an uncle she had never heard of had left her his house in Mauritius.

It was incredible. It was unbelievable. It should have excited her, except that nothing did these days. For the last two months she had lived in a state of limbo, caring little what went on in the outside world, wrapped in her own tight sphere of misery, despite attempts by many of her college friends to snap her out of this lethargy.

Amie's mother had died three years earlier when Amie was just sixteen. Her father had remarried within six months, much to her disgust, and she had immediately left home in York and headed for London, fortunate enough to find that the college was still prepared to take her, despite the fact that she had written cancelling her application

when her mother died. She had thought her father
would need her at home and had been prepared
to give up all thoughts of a career for his sake, until
he had shown that he was perfectly capable of managing his own life.

It had hurt, his marrying again so quickly. She
could not believe that he had so easily forgotten
her mother after eighteen years of marriage. Her
mother had been French, an easily excitable woman
from whom Amie had inherited her quick temper
and flashing green eyes. Her thick black hair was all
she had in common with her father, and Amie had
had an unholy row with him before leaving York.

She had not written since, just a card at Christ-
mas and on his birthdays. It had come as a surprise,
this letter, and before she opened it she had been
trying to think what he could possibly be writing
to her about.

An inheritance was the last thought on her mind.
Her mother had never mentioned having a brother,
yet he must have known all about her, otherwise
why would he have remembered her in his will?
Philippe Duval, according to her father's letter,
and he had given her the name and address of a
lawyer in London who would give her full information if she contacted them.

Mauritius! She did not even know where it
was. Curiosity began to take the place of indifference and with a sense of purpose she fetched
from the bookcase an old school atlas, one of the
few possessions she had brought with her from
York. Mauritius, a tiny island in the Indian Ocean,
five hundred miles east of Madagascar, size seven

hundred and twenty square miles, capital, Port Louis.

It would be warm there, nothing like the rain and snow they were experiencing in London at the moment. She looked out of the window. The sky was blue, but according to the weather forecast rain was promised later, and there were still a few drifts of snow against the hedges in neighbouring gardens. People were scurrying past with their collars turned up, hands deep in pockets. It was cold, despite the sun, and the wind tossed a handful of litter in the gutter, sweet papers, empty paper bags, all manner of bits and pieces left by people who queued for the bus outside.

Amie had been lucky to get this flat. Mrs Hobbs was recently widowed and she and Ginny Jones were her first tenants. The woman had been terribly upset over the accident and had since treated Amie more as a daughter than a lodger, popping in each day to make sure she was all right, chiding her for not getting out more.

A tap on the door told Amie that Mrs Hobbs was paying her usual morning call. 'Come in,' she invited, 'the door's open.'

Her landlady was a warm, friendly woman with a plain face and lank reddish-brown hair. She raised her brows when she saw the open atlas. 'Going somewhere, lovey? That's right, it will do you good. A holiday's what you need right now, take your mind off—you know...' She seemed vaguely embarrassed and tailed off awkwardly. 'Where is it you're thinking of going?'

'Not a holiday, Hobby,' said Amie fondly. 'As a matter of fact I've been left some property—in

Mauritius of all places. I was just looking where it was—not that I intend going, but I might sell. I could do with the money until I decide what I'm going to do now that——' It was her turn to leave a sentence unfinished.

'I understand, love,' said Mrs Hobbs, busying herself putting on the kettle and reaching out cups and the tea caddy. 'But I think you're wrong. At least go and look at the place. You never know, you might fall in love with it and decide to spend the rest of your life there. My Fred used to talk about Mauritius, what was it he called it—jewel of the Indian Ocean. Went there as a young man, before we met, always promised to take me, but what with one thing and another we could never afford it. It's sugar they grow there—green fields of waving sugar-cane. It's a beautiful place, Amie.'

Despite misgivings Hobby's enthusiasm aroused Amie's interest, and she nodded her head slowly. 'I suppose it would do no harm to take a look. It was my mother's brother who owned it, Uncle Philippe. Apparently I'm his only living relative and although we've never met he left me his house.'

'That was very kind of him,' said Mrs Hobbs, making the tea and joining Amie at the table. 'And just what you need right now. Couldn't have come at a better time.'

'I've got to ring the lawyers,' said Amie slowly. 'They have all the information.'

'Then do it now,' said the older woman, 'no sense in waiting. Here, give me the number, I'll dial it for you.'

'I can manage,' said Amie defensively. 'I'm not completely useless.' The moment she said the words she regretted them, but the slightest reference to her hand irritated her and she could not help reacting as she did. Everyone thought she was putting it on, and humoured her, and she wasn't! She just couldn't use it—God knows, she had tried often enough.

She lifted the receiver and placed it on the table beside the telephone while she dialled the number. This was one thing she had become expert at, dialling with her left hand—if only drawing was so simple she would have no problem.

Atkinson, Atkinson & Pollard would discuss nothing over the phone, so she made an appointment to call in and see them that same afternoon. The more she thought about leaving behind cold damp England, and all the unhappy memories it held for her, the more excited Amie became, and by the time she left the flat later that same day she had made up her mind to fly out to Mauritius.

The island was all that Hobby had said it would be, jewel of the Indian Ocean, an emerald on a bed of blue velvet. As the plane lost height Amie made out its pear shape, the switchback mountains shrouded by mist, green fields, pale gleaming sands, and the thin white line of foam over the fringe of coral reefs which encircled it.

Now that her long journey was almost over she could not contain a quiver of apprehension. No one knew she was arriving; she had not written, not really knowing whom to contact. Mr Atkinson had told her that her late uncle's manager had been left the bulk of his estate, the house only coming to her. She was half inclined to sell, because there was no way she could afford to keep the house, although Hobby had assured her she would be so enchanted with the island she would never want to leave.

They landed at Plaisance Airport and in no time at all Amie found herself through passport control. Her apprehension increased as she made her way to the line of waiting taxis. It was no use trying to delude herself that she was not concerned as to what sort of reception she would get. But she soon forgot her natural fear with so much new and interesting on which to feast her eyes. The villages through which they passed teemed with people of all nationalities—Indians, Créoles, French, English, Chinese, and the rainbow hues of their dress added colour and excitement to the scene.

Already Amie's artistic mind was conjuring up new fabric designs and textures based on this jungle of colour, and it was a few minutes before she realised that these ideas could never be carried out.

She subsided into her seat. This was the first time since the accident that she had forgotten about her injury, and it distressed her beyond measure to think that she was unable to take advantage of these wonderful surroundings.

They passed through acres and acres of cane-fields with their piles of volcanic rock heaped to one side out of the way of the machinery which would ultimately cut the cane. Amie had read that Mauritius was a volcanic island, but had not expected to see quite so much evidence.

The changing scenery entranced her, as Hobby had said it would—wandering rivers, moonscapish peaks, towns, fields, forests, bizarre-shaped mount-tains. It was all so different from anything she had ever known—weird and wonderful, and she should be on top of the world—so why wasn't she?

Was it fear of the unknown, having no idea what to expect, what she would find? Or was it because she was tired, desperately tired? She had been travelling for over fourteen hours, having taken off from Heathrow at ten the previous evening. Counting the fact that she had had to put her watch forward four hours upon arrival it made it almost five o'clock. She wondered whether it was worth it.

The lawyer had been unable to tell her very much about her uncle's activities, except that he owned a sugar estate and had died a very rich man. When she mentioned Philippe Duval's name the taxi driver had nodded immediately, confirming that he had been well known on the island.

It did not take long to reach the house, less than an hour in fact, and after the long flight it seemed to Amie only minutes. But whatever she had expected it had been nothing like this. 'Are you sure this is Shangri-La?' she asked her taxi driver in French. It was fortunate she knew the language, for it seemed to be spoken by everyone, even though she had been informed that English was the official language.

'Quite sure, *mademoiselle*.' His gleaming white smile was in much evidence as he announced how much the journey had cost. Amie was astounded, sure that because she had confessed to being a relative of the wealthy man he had doubled his price. With a sigh she handed over the necessary number of rupees and stood beside her luggage which the still grinning driver had unloaded in front of the house.

House! It was more like a mansion. As she faced it it spread away on either side of her, a portico running its entire length, a splendid Colonial-style house with countless windows and an immense front door reached by a flight of stone steps.

She left her cases where they were and mounted the steps with increasing trepidation. If there was no answer, what then? Maybe she ought to have asked the taxi-driver to wait until she had made sure. The house was miles from anywhere, set in its own spacious grounds, and she felt too tired to do any chasing around. Perhaps it had not been such a good idea to arrive unannounced.

But she need not have worried; the door opened before she had even reached it, and she was confronted by a big, powerful-looking man with a tan as deep as mahogany and a shock of sun-bleached hair. Keen blue eyes regarded her and her luggage suspiciously.

'Yes?'

The word was curt to the point of rudeness and Amie was immediately on the defensive. Whoever he was this man had no right here—not in her house. 'Who are you?' she asked, instilling an equally cold response into her voice.

'I don't see that it has anything to do with you.' The wide mouth hardened and he folded his arms across his chest. Muscular arms, she noted, strong and sinewy, as though he did plenty of hard manual labour.

Was he one of the workers on her uncle's estate? If so what was he doing here in his—no, *her* house?

'It is every business of mine,' she said distantly.
'I happen to be the new owner and I demand to
know what you are doing here.'

His face lightened fractionally, though there was
no softening of those piercing blue eyes. They were
like twin shafts of steel driving through her and if
she hadn't been so sure of her ground Amie would
have wilted beneath his gaze. Instead she returned
his stare evenly, her chin tilting, waiting to see
what his response to her statement would be.

'So you are Amie Douglas? I'd begun to wonder
whether we would ever see you.'

'I've no idea what you mean by that remark,'
she said tightly, 'but don't you think it would be
a good idea if we talked inside?'

He stood back. 'My apologies,' and the mocking voice belied his words.

'My luggage,' she said haughtily. 'Would you
mind?'

His eyes narrowed, but he brushed past her and
effortlessly picked up the two cases. Again Amie
was aware of his strength. It had been all she could
do to lift them herself, her whole wardrobe and
several books were squashed inside, yet he handled
them with as much ease as if they were empty.

The square hall in which she found herself was
tiled in marble mosaic and when he dropped her
cases the sound echoed up the wide staircase at the
other end. It was not a large hall, but impressive,
the almost white walls hung with various tapestries
and sculptured pictures in bronze and brass.

Trying to make it look as though owning a house
was something that came natural to her. Amie
opened the first door and swept inside, observing

briefly the huge desk littered with papers and the booklined walls before turning to confront the big man who had followed her into the room.

He beckoned her to sit down and then, as if *he* owned the place, he took the seat behind the desk, selecting a cheroot from an ebony box which he lit with a matching lighter. He then tilted back his chair and put his feet up on the desk, watching her shrewdly through the thin haze of smoke. His chiselled mouth was grim and forbidding and the blue eyes arrogantly aloof. He was not a type she had come up against before, and although they had done no more than exchange a few words she felt instinctively that she couldn't trust him an inch.

She moved uncomfortably in her seat, not liking the way he was insolently studying her. It was as though he was mentally assessing her and she had the firm impression that he found her lacking in whatever it was he was looking for.

She crossed one leg over the other and tugged down her skirt. 'Perhaps you wouldn't mind telling me who you are, Mr—er——?'

'Oliver Maxwell,' he said easily, 'and in case you're wondering exactly where I fit in, I was your uncle's manager before he died.'

Amie nodded. 'I believe you inherited his estate,' she returned drily, the picture suddenly becoming clear. 'But not his house, so what are you doing here?'

'Someone needed to look after the place,' he countered brusquely, 'while the lawyers were searching for you. I can't imagine why Philippe left you the place since you never bothered to visit him, nor even had the courtesy to write.'

Amie could have told him that she had not known of her uncle's existence, but she did not see why she should explain to a complete stranger. 'That is my business,' she said primly. 'The fact remains that I'm here now—so you are at liberty to return to your own house. I presume that you do have somewhere to live, that you didn't stay here with my uncle?' She had suddenly made up her mind that she was not going to sell, and for some inexplicable reason her decision had something to do with the man sitting opposite.

'Oh, I have a place,' he returned evenly. 'A two-roomed shack not half a mile from here.'

'Which you decided wasn't good enough for you, after you'd inherited the estate?' Amie eyed him coldly. 'A pity, Mr Maxwell. I'm sorry if I've spoiled your—er—taste of luxury, but now I'm here there'll be no need for you to remain.'

If she had thought to put him in his place she was mistaken. Eyebrows a slight shade darker than his hair rose mockingly. 'Don't get me wrong, Miss Douglas, I like my home, I find it infinitely more easy to run than this place. Think you'll be able to manage?' Again the blue eyes regarded her clinically. 'You're very young, younger than I imagined——'

'But not entirely incapable,' cut in Amie heatedly, 'if that's what you're insinuating. I've not exactly been mollycoddled. I left home over four years ago and I've managed quite well since then.'

'Living in a bedsitter, I presume?' A wry twist to his lips. 'A far cry from all this.'

And recalling the palace-like proportions she had seen from outside Amie was inclined to agree.

'But if you're quite sure,' he swung his legs lazily down, 'I'll go—now. Goodbye, Miss Douglas, good luck.'

She had not expected this and was tempted to call him back, to beg him to at least give her some insight into the running of the house, all that it entailed. She did not know the first thing about it, the layout, whether there was any help or whether whatever staff there had been had gone when her uncle died.

But pride forbade her. She wanted no help from *him*. He was insufferable—rude, arrogant, pompous, acting as though he owned the place! No doubt he wished he did. Perhaps he had expected the house as well as the estate and had secretly hoped she would never turn up.

It amazed her that he had gone so readily, but she did not dwell on it; all that concerned her was that she get some sleep. She had temporarily forgotten her tiredness, but now it came sweeping back and without bothering to explore she climbed the marble staircase, tugging one suitcase as best she could, the other she left where it was.

A lengthy corridor confronted her at the top, running, it appeared, the entire length of the house. The first door revealed a linen cupboard, well stocked and faintly redolent of lavender. A nice touch, she thought, something she had not expected out here on this tropical island.

Several of the rooms had their furniture covered in dust sheets, but at length she found one that looked as though it was kept in readiness for unexpected guests. She opened her suitcase and dragged out a nightdress and despite the fact that it was only a little after seven she undressed, quickly washed in the adjoining bathroom, and climbed wearily into bed.

She fell asleep almost at once, only to wake with a start two hours later feeling the hair prickle at the back of her neck, wondering what it was that had woken her. She lay perfectly still, listening intently, ready to scream at the first sign of an intruder.

Of course it could be someone else who lived in the house, she reasoned, it had been silly not to check before she came to bed. But she had been so tired. Now she was wide awake—and frightened, more frightened than she had ever been in her life. The darkness made matters worse. When the door opened, revealing a huge shadowy figure, she screamed and felt her blood run cold, pulling the sheets over her head as she used to when a child suffering from a bad dream.

'What the hell?'

A well remembered voice cut into the silence and Amie thrust back the sheets and sat up, her black hair ruffled attractively. 'You!' she accused coldly, relief sharpening her voice. 'What are you doing here?'

'I could ask the same of you. Was it coincidence or perhaps wishful thinking that made you choose my room?' He came inside and closed the door, switching on the light before leaning back against the wall regarding her with that lazy insolent expression to which she was becoming accustomed.

Amie shot out of bed, heedless of the fact that she was wearing a see-through nightdress. 'Your bed? God, if I'd known I'd have gone to the other end of the house!'

Her words appeared to amuse him and his eyes skimmed her slim shapely body, 'I'd share my bed with you any time.'

'Is that why you came back?' She looked quickly for something to cover herself, but her case was still packed and she decided it would be too undignified to rummage through her belongings. Tilting her head proudly, she tried to pretend it did not matter, that she always went around wearing revealing clothes.

What did worry her was his motive for returning. They appeared to be the only two people in the house; if he took it into his head to make advances there was little she could do to stop him. She would be pitifully weak against the strength in that powerful body. She took a long look at his muscular frame, wide shoulders tapering to slim hips, tan denim trousers hugging his thighs, rubber-soled canvas shoes—just right for creeping about the house! She returned to his face, handsome in a rugged kind of way, but too superior for her liking. She hated him and glared fiercely, green eyes flashing. 'Are you going to answer my question?'

'I'd be more interested to hear what you make of me.'

She hadn't realised he had been watching her. 'Not much,' she said tightly. 'I don't go for men who burst their way into bedrooms uninvited.'

The thick brows lifted cynically. 'You're reading more into this situation than there is, lady. As I said, this was my room, and I merely came to pick up some belongings.'

'You expect me to believe that?'

'Believe what you like, it's the truth, though perhaps I would be a fool not to take advantage of the situation. It's been a long time since I kissed a pretty English girl.'

'And it will be even longer if I have anything to do with it,' announced Amie, backing round to the other side of the bed as he came across the room. He had the lithe, easy grace of a wild animal, a predator about to catch its prey, eyes narrowed and watchful, a sinister curl to his lips. She felt more afraid now that she had when she saw him shadowed in the doorway.

CHAPTER TWO

'You touch me,' shrieked Amie, 'and I'll——'

'What? Scream again? It will make no difference, there's no one to hear. You're entirely at my mercy, dear lady.' Oliver Maxwell took another step nearer and Amie looked anxiously around for something with which to protect herself.

A vase on the dresser was within easy reach and without stopping to think she reached out, only to find it slipping from her fingers. It crashed noisily, cracking the glass top of the dresser and breaking into dozens of tiny pieces.

'Clumsy young fool, I wouldn't have hurt you.'

His eyes were angry now. 'Your uncle had many treasured possessions, that vase among them—it was over a hundred years old.'

'Then it should have been locked away,' snapped Amie, rubbing her fingers and wondering how she could have been so stupid as to forget the accident which had robbed them of all feeling.

'Have you hurt your hand?' he asked sharply. 'Here, let me take a look.'

Amie did not want him to touch her. 'It's nothing, something that happened before I came out here.'

'I'd still prefer to see it,' he said tightly. 'One can't afford to ignore cuts in this heat,' and before she could stop him he had lifted her arm. It was too late then to hide the disfiguring scar which ran from elbow to wrist. He drew in his breath tightly and frowned. 'Some accident! What happened?'

She shrugged and snatching back her arm hid it behind her back. 'A car crash,' she said, trying to sound indifferent, 'not that I consider it any business of yours. Would you mind getting whatever it is you came for so I can go back to sleep. I've had a very long, tiring journey, in case you didn't realise.'

The pale blue eyes glittered hatefully. 'Really? Something tells me that you won't get back to sleep for a long time. How about joining me for a drink?'

Amie met his gaze coldly. 'No, thanks, Mr Maxwell. In any case, aren't you forgetting that you have no right in this house now? If anyone does the inviting it should be me.'

'And that is something you are hardly likely to

do.' His lips curled into a sneering smile. 'Not a very friendly creature, are you? You're not going to get yourself liked very much, not with that attitude.'

She would have liked to tell him that her attitude depended very much upon the person she was with, but wisely decided it would not do to anger him further. She would be completely at his mercy if he took it into his head to take offence at anything she said. 'I treat as I find,' she returned tightly, not quite managing to hide the hatred she felt.

He noticed and his eyes narrowed. 'I get your meaning, but if you thought I would welcome Philippe's unknown niece with open arms you were mistaken.'

'Because you wanted the house as well as the estate?' She could not help it, the words were out before she could stop them.

'So that's what you think?' The proud head tilted arrogantly. 'Would you believe me if I said you were wrong, Miss Douglas, that my interest is purely in the production of sugar, and that home comforts mean no more to me than a place to eat and sleep?'

She returned his gaze guardedly, uneasily aware that he could be speaking the truth, but not prepared to admit it. 'No, I wouldn't,' she said firmly. 'You don't strike me as the sort to put up with anything less than the best, even your clothes shriek money. If you would have me believe that material things don't matter why aren't you dressed in rags?'

A thunderous frown darkened his face, the blue eyes chips of ice. 'I think you've gone far enough, miss. I'm quite sure that if your uncle had known the type of person you are he would have had second thoughts about leaving you his house.'

'Uncle Philippe didn't know me at all.'

'He heard of you, though, through your mother. They corresponded regularly, didn't she tell you? He thought the world of you, did Philippe; it seems you must have changed since your mother died, unless she was feeding him a pack of lies.'

'My mother would never do that,' cried Amie defensively. 'She had no reason. I'm quite sure she never knew what he intended doing, otherwise she would have told me.'

'Not necessarily. Monique didn't know she would die so young. Maybe she had her own interests at heart, maybe she thought the whole family would benefit. A pity your father married again, otherwise he might have been out here with you.'

Amie was furious at the disparaging way he spoke. 'How dare you! What right have you to talk about my parents like that—and how do you know so much?'

He smiled, an infuriatingly insolent smile. 'Philippe and I were very close, we were more like friends than employer and employee. I know everything about you, honey, or at least I did, until Monique died. After that, nothing. Philippe wrote to your father once or twice but never received a reply, so he stopped trying in the end. I had no idea he still regarded you with affection, and I was as surprised as you must have been when he remembered you in his will.'

'I bet you were!' she snapped violently. 'Disappointed too, I expect.'

A curious smile curved his lips. 'He wasn't quite

so stupid as all that, was he?' He folded his arms and studied her curiously. 'He's left you the house, but no means of keeping it. What are your plans, Miss Spitfire Douglas?'

'I shall manage.' Her words were quiet and determined, not for anything would she give him the satisfaction of knowing that this was the one thing worrying her.

'You might have to sell.' A gleam of pleasure in the blue eyes.

'I doubt it, even if I have to take a job myself to pay for it.'

'With a crippled hand?'

If anything had been calculated to hurt, it was this. Her cheeks flamed and her green eyes flashed and she felt like crying. She took a deep breath and said tightly, 'So you've noticed, but that's not the end of everything, is it? My brain still functions perfectly well and I've another hand, I can teach myself to use that.'

'Then why haven't you?' he asked sharply. 'You instinctively picked that vase up with your right hand, knowing full well what would happen. Have you been feeling too damn sorry for yourself to learn to use your other one? It's not a recent thing, this accident, the scar tells me that. Time enough, I would have supposed, to allow you to teach yourself to do things with your left hand.'

She eyed him angrily and refused to speak.

'What was it Monique told your uncle you were going to college for? Fashion designing, wasn't it, or something like that. Have you thrown it all by the board, Amie Douglas, is that why you came out here, because you'd decided your whole life was in ruins?'

He was so right, damn him. 'Get out,' she cried furiously. 'Get out!' He was too perceptive by far. Those discerning eyes and that keen brain, he had weighed her up from the beginning and knew as much about her as she did herself. She hated him. With every fibre of her being she hated him, but of one thing she was sure, he was not going to turn her out of this house. She would find some way of keeping it on. Quite how evaded her at this moment, but she was certainly not going to be beaten by this insufferable man.

'Don't you like being told the truth?' He made no attempt to move, eyes watching her lazily, a contemptuous curl to his lips. 'Does it hurt, almost as much as your arm did after the accident?'

When she refused to reply he turned and disappeared. Amie listened until his footsteps faded and the banging of the front door told her that she had the house to herself again.

She threw herself limply on to the bed and closed her eyes. The scene had left her shattered, yet she knew she would not sleep. Never before had she met anyone quite like Oliver Maxwell. Perhaps after tonight he would keep out of her way. She hoped so, she really did.

When sleep eventually claimed Amie it was blessed relief. He had disturbed her, this man, in a way that she found exasperating. It was not his looks, that was for sure; her ideal was tall, dark and handsome, not a giant blond as hard as nails and with about as much regard for her feelings as she might have had for an insect that she ground beneath her heel. It had to be his chemistry, his physical make-up—and to her horror she found herself wondering what it would be like to be kissed by him. He would not be a tender lover, that much she knew. He was a hard, passionate man and his lovemaking would be equally fervid and demonstrative.

Fortunately she fell asleep before her thoughts went any further and when she woke the next morning she had forgotten these unbidden fantasies, her only memory being of the man who had angered her so greatly.

A tap on her door made her heartbeats accelerate and she drew the sheets up to her chin before calling tentatively, 'W-who is it?'

It couldn't be him. He wouldn't dare. Or would he? She would put nothing past Oliver Maxwell.

The Créole girl who entered was such a contrast that Amie grinned in relief, not even bothering to wonder where she had come from or whether she had witnessed anything of what had happened last night.

'*Bonjour*,' she said automatically, looking at the tray in the girl's hand. 'Is that for me?'

The girl nodded and smiled, showing even white teeth. She wore a short skirt and a low-cut blouse, black curling hair topped her enchanting pretty face and gold hoops adorned her ears. She was about sixteen and very aware of her sexual advantages, and Amie guessed she would know exactly how to put them to good use.

Her hips swayed as she crossed the room with the breakfast tray, and Amie could not help wondering what sort of treatment Oliver Maxwell got from this precocious young girl. Perhaps this was the sort he liked? He had certainly made it clear that he was not attracted so far as Amie was concerned.

Amie took the tray and settled it on her knees. 'How did you know I was here?'

'Monsieur Maxwell sent me up,' replied the foreign girl politely.

'How kind of him.' Amie's dryness was lost. 'Did you work for my uncle, is there any other help in the house?'

She shook her head, dark curls bobbing. 'I did work here, but not now. After Monsieur Duval died there was no need.'

'But didn't Oliver Maxwell move in?' asked Amie, feeling the need to satisfy her curiosity, in case he hadn't been telling her the truth.

'Not permanently,' said the girl, much to Amie's disgust. 'He used to come up sometimes, to make sure it was all right and to do any necessary paperwork, the rest of the time he spent at his own place. I work for him there.' She said this last sentence proudly and with an unconscious provocative movement of her body. Each to his own kind, thought Amie unkindly, not fully realising just why she should think such a thing, except that to her it sounded ludicrous that he should need help in the house when he had said it was nothing more than a two-roomed shack.

'Monsieur Maxwell says that I am to stay here and help you,' continued the Créole girl. 'Are you going to be here very long, Miss Douglas?'

Was that what he had told her, that she would be returning to England as soon as she had had time to sort out her uncle's affairs? Amie's lips firmed.

'I intend making this my home, I thought he knew that. Perhaps he was under a misapprehension. If you'd still like to stay I should be grateful, though I shan't be able to pay you very much.' Indeed she couldn't really afford to pay the girl at all, but she needed someone; there was no way she could manage this big house by herself.

The girl nodded. 'That is all right. Monsieur Maxwell said that he himself would pay my wages.'

Amie's chin shot up. The nerve of the man! She could imagine the condescending way in which he had said it. She looked crossly at the girl. 'What's your name?' she asked.

'Peta.'

'Well, Peta, you can tell Mr Maxwell from me that I don't want any charity. This is my house and if you work for me *I* shall pay you.'

'As you wish, Miss Douglas.' The girl was clearly puzzled and Amie began to wish she had not been quite so hasty. Why shouldn't he pay? He could afford it better than she. But now that she had spoken she could not change her mind. It would make her look a fool and no doubt Peta would repeat everything that had been said.

As the girl made to leave the room Amie said, 'Oh, Peta, I left one of my suitcases in the hall, do you think you could manage to bring it up?'

'It's outside, miss,' said the coloured girl at once. 'Monsieur Maxwell must have brought it up when he came last night. If that is all I will go and start work in the kitchen.'

Amie let her go, staring absently at the bacon and egg on her plate. How had Peta known he came here last night? Was she his confidante as well as his lover? Was Peta as jealous of her as she was becoming of Peta? Had it been the girl's own idea to come up here today, see for herself what the newcomer looked like, satisfy her own curiosity? Perhaps they had had a laugh over her last night, no doubt Oliver Maxwell had exaggerated their meeting and told the young seductress in no uncertain terms exactly what he thought of the girl from England who had come to stake her claim.

Amie's breakfast lay untouched. She pushed the tray away and climbed out of bed. She took a quick, cold, invigorating shower, already beginning to feel the heat of the day, then tucked a towel round her and unpacked her cases, thrusting her clothes untidily into drawers, selecting a long-sleeved cotton dress to wear now.

She brushed her short straight hair, flicking back the ends from her face. It had been long before the accident and just for a moment she regretted having it cut, but it had been difficult to manage one-handed. She contemplated making up her face and then decided against it. In this heat it wouldn't last anyway. She left her bed, Peta could make that later.

The tray she managed in one hand and then found her way down to the kitchen. It was through a door beneath the stairs and had been easy to find because Peta was singing loudly enough to be heard all over the house.

'You have not eaten,' she accused as soon as Amie appeared with the fully laden tray. 'You did not like it?'

'I wasn't hungry. What are you doing now?'

'Preparing lunch,' said the Créole girl readily.

Amie looked at the rice and the curry, sniffing the highly spiced seasonings, and wondered how she could tell her that she preferred English food without hurting her feelings. But before she could speak Peta continued:

'Monsieur Maxwell is coming up to the house for lunch today. He asked me to tell you. He said there were things that you had to discuss.'

Such as what? thought Amie, but she said nothing. He was taking a whole lot for granted, was Oliver Maxwell. She needed no help from him and the sooner he realised it the better. This was her house now and he had no part in it.

'I see,' she said flatly. 'While you're doing that I think I'll take a look over the house. I was tired yesterday.'

Many of the rooms on the ground floor were also shrouded in dust sheets, making Amie wonder why her uncle had bothered to keep on such a big house. Why hadn't he bought something smaller, something more suited to the taste of a man living alone? What rooms were in use, though, were magnificent, expensively furnished and filled with art treasures that in themselves were worth a small fortune—and they were all hers!

It was unbelievable. If she was short of money she only had to sell some of this stuff, but she knew she couldn't, that wasn't what her uncle wanted. He had known she was set on a career in the fashion industry. Maybe he had thought, as she had when she first arrived, that the colours and exotic surroundings here would inspire her. What he hadn't known was the accident, of course. There was absol-

utely no way now that she would be able to fulfil
her ambition.

Unless, of course, she painstakingly taught herself to use her left hand. Oliver Maxwell's words
had hurt, more than she cared to admit. It was one
thing to know herself that she was being a martyr,
but to have it forcibly driven home by someone as
hateful as him was something else.

She was not looking forward one little bit to
lunching with him, conscious that it would not be
a pleasurable occasion. She could go out, explore
the grounds, but Peta would tell him and he would
know she had done it on purpose.

By lunchtime she had composed herself and
greeted him coolly, trying to forget their encounter
last night when he had accused her of feeling sorry
for herself.

'How did you sleep?' he asked, a wry twist to his
lips.

His eyes were bluer than she remembered, his
hair bleached almost white by the sun. He wore
blue denims today and a white, short-sleeved shirt
which emphasised his deep tan and revealed his
sinewy arms.

'Very well,' she lied, hoping he would not notice
the shadows beneath her eyes.

He did, of course, he was that type of man, watching her narrowly before he changed the subject. 'I
trust Peta is looking after you satisfactorily?'

Amie inclined her head. 'There was no need, I
could have managed.'

His lips flickered. 'I'm not so sure. In this heat,
looking after this house, you'd be exhausted after

a few days—especially having to do everything one-handed.'

She guessed this was calculated to hurt, and it did. She flushed angrily. 'There was no need for that, Mr Maxwell! I know my own capabilities. And I'll pay Peta myself.'

His shrug was brief enough to be hardly discernible, and when the Créole girl came in with two dishes of iced soup they exchanged looks, the youngster's dark eyes flashing provocatively, her whole body moving with deliberate sensuality as she left the room.

He watched her until she had gone and then turned back to Amie. 'Call me Oliver. Mr Maxwell's far too formal, don't you agree, if we're to be friends?'

'I'm not sure that I want to be friends with you, Mr Maxwell,' she said directly, taking a spoonful of soup with a hand that was not entirely steady. It was delicious, but she was so conscious of her companion watching that she drank no more than a few mouthfuls.

He was deliberately making her aware of her inadequacy, and it rankled, made her hate him more than ever, if that was possible. He really was the most disagreeable man she had ever met.

When Peta returned for their dishes she pouted sulkily. 'You do not like my soup?'

And Amie, anxious not to upset this girl who, against her wishes, was compelled to help in this house, said quickly, 'Oh, yes, it's delicious, but I'm really not very hungry. It must be the heat.'

'You had no breakfast,' accused Peta, stacking

the dishes neatly and shooting a triumphant look at Oliver as if expecting him to say something.

He frowned, but that was all, though Amie suspected he would be watching her eating habits closely from now on.

She actually was hungry by this time, having eaten little on the journey yesterday and nothing at all so far today. One taste of the curry, though, was enough to convince her that she couldn't possibly eat it. The hot spices burnt her mouth and she gulped down a glass of cold water after only one mouthful of the inflammable food.

Oliver looked amused. 'I'm afraid Peta's a little heavy-handed with the cayenne pepper and pimento, you'll get used to it.'

'No, I won't,' she spluttered. 'I refuse to eat it. If that's all she can cook then I'll do my own. You can have her back—I'm sure your need of her is greater than mine.'

The implication was unmistakable and his smile quickly disappeared. 'Get your facts right before you make any more cracks like that,' he said harshly.

'I'm only drawing my own conclusions from what Peta has inferred,' she returned evenly.

'They're wrong,' he shot back. 'Eat your curry and let's have no more of this nonsense.'

She pushed her plate away. 'I don't want it, it's entirely unpalatable.'

'You must eat,' he protested, 'you're already too thin.' He studied the pale, almost translucent skin across her high cheekbones, her straight tip-tilted nose and the slender column of her throat. All else was covered by her dress and she was unaware that it revealed with tantalising clarity to the man opposite the pointed roundness of her breasts.

'You want the sun on that arm,' he said abruptly, 'the scar will fade far more quickly than if you keep it covered—besides, it's far too hot to wear something like that.'

'What would you suggest?' she asked drily, 'a bikini?'

His eyes glinted. 'Not a bad idea, but perhaps not entirely practical. What are you afraid of, that people might cringe at the sight of it? It's not all that bad. You yourself probably think it's worse than it really is.'

To her it was a memory, a vivid memory of that fateful night when Ginny died. Perhaps she didn't want it to fade, perhaps she subconsciously relished the idea of having this constant, haunting reminder. It was her way of punishing herself.

She didn't answer him, selecting an apple from the bowl of fruit in the centre of the table and biting into it with her small white teeth. 'What was it you came to discuss, Mr Maxwell?' and her eyes were hard and bright, hating him with an intenseness she found disturbing.

He continued eating his curry with relish, pausing between mouthfuls to say, 'I thought you might like to know where your uncle kept his papers, how much it costs to run Shangri-La, and a few other details that are your concern now you're the new owner. Did you know, for instance, that Philippe held a party here once a year for all his workers? Quite some party, that, and I happen to know they're all hoping you will carry on the tradition.'

He must have known she could not afford it and

his brilliant blue eyes watched closely for her reaction. She stiffened resolutely. 'It's too soon yet for
me to make such decisions, as you well know, and
if all the papers are in my uncle's study there's no
need for you to go through them with me. I can
work things out for myself.'

'Clever girl,' came the sarcastic response, 'but
they're not quite like the accounts you've probably
been used to. I would still prefer to show you.'

'Then we may as well get it over with now,' she
said abruptly, standing and dropping her half-eaten
apple on to the table.

'I've not finished my lunch yet,' he said coldly.
'Sit down and don't be silly. Peta will bring in coffee
in a moment.'

Almost as though on cue the dark girl entered,
setting down an elegant silver coffee pot and dainty
china cups. Amie poured the coffee. 'How do you
like it?' she asked distantly.

'Black, no sugar. Why don't you finish your
apple?'

Because she was hungry she did so, not because
he had asked her. Then she drank her coffee and
sat waiting impatiently for him to finish. He took
his time and she was fuming when he eventually
pushed back his chair. 'Peta's a good cook,' he said
in a satisfied sort of voice. 'I shall miss her.'

'That's your bad luck,' she returned bitterly, wondering whether he was hinting that she should invite him up here since he had gone to the trouble of
loaning her his servant.

'I'm not complaining,' he returned evenly. 'I'm
quite an expert myself, if need be. You must come
to dinner some time.'

Fortunately he did not seem to require an answer or Amie might have been tempted to suggest that he might try to poison her, so that he could lay claim to the house himself.

Her uncle's books were well kept and she was relieved to see that everything was paid up to date, but she was aghast to learn exactly how much it required to run a place this size. Admittedly all the staff had left, and she intended trying to struggle along with just Peta for the time being, but the gardener still did his work—she had noticed when she came the immaculate lawns and well-tended flower beds, and his wage was generous to say the least.

She pointed this out to Oliver. 'He had a choice,' he replied, 'of either living in one of your uncle's houses rent free and receiving a low wage, or keeping on his own house and getting more money. He settled for the latter.' He looked at her, his eyes gleaming with cynical amusement. 'You're not thinking of getting rid of him and doing the gardens yourself?'

'I'm not that foolish,' she replied heatedly.

'But you don't see how you'll be able to afford to keep him on?'

'It's an expense I could do without,' she admitted. 'I wonder why my uncle left me the house and no money.'

He grinned insolently. 'Perhaps he thought you and I might get together.'

Her eyes widened. 'You mean that we might——' She couldn't put it into words, it was too ludicrous. She wouldn't marry Oliver Maxwell if he was the last man on earth!

'I agree with you,' he said, as though reading her thoughts. 'It wouldn't work, you're not my type either. I prefer someone with a little warmth, someone who has regard for her family, not someone who neglects them scandalously but comes running immediately she thinks there'll be some financial benefit.'

'You swine!' cried Amie. 'When I heard of my uncle's death it was too late to get here.'

'I don't mean his funeral,' he said drily, 'that of necessity had to be quick because of the heat, but how about all the years in between, not so much as a card saying how are you, Uncle?'

Amie's lips thinned. He wasn't worth arguing with, he would clearly think only what he wanted. 'I don't have to take this from you,' she said frigidly. 'If you've finished you can go.'

'But I haven't finished,' he said coolly, 'and that's the second time you've told me to get out of this house. I don't think I like it.'

'And I don't like you here,' she said, 'and as the house is legally mine you haven't a leg to stand on.'

'I'll make you an offer,' he said bluntly. 'I'll buy the house.'

She stared at him for a second or two. Wasn't that what she had wanted in the first place, hadn't it been what she told Hobby she intended doing? Why then was she hesitating? The answer was clear—had it been any other man she might have agreed, but not to Oliver Maxwell, not in a hundred years.

'It's no deal,' she said coldly. 'I intend staying whether you like it or not. Now will you go?'

His jaw firmed and for a long moment he eyed

her grimly. Then with a brief shrug he turned. He
did not speak again, he left the house and she was
alone, perversely wishing that she had not been so
rude. It was going to get mighty lonely out here
with no one but Peta for company.

CHAPTER THREE

IT was a week before Amie saw Oliver again, seven
days during which she had accustomed herself to
the house, the heat, and above all the fact that the
little money she had saved would not last as long as
she had at first imagined.

He came uninvited and announced that he was
staying to dinner. Amie greeted him coldly, despite
the fact that deep down she was pleased to see him.
It had become unbearably lonely. The house itself
was miles from anywhere and although she had gone
for long walks she had met no one and spoken to
no one other than Peta and the gardener.

'How are you getting on?' he asked pleasantly,
crossing to the drinks cupboard and pouring himself a Scotch.

'Help yourself,' she said pointedly, resenting the
way he made himself at home. He might have done
before, when her uncle was alive, but that didn't
give him the right to do it now.

'Counting the cost already, are we?' he sneered.

Digging into the pocket of his superbly cut grey slacks, he pulled out a handful of coins and tossed them on to the table. 'I think that should cover it.'

Savagely Amie swept them to the floor. 'I don't want your money, but politeness doesn't cost anything. Next time perhaps you'll wait until *I* offer you a drink.'

Surprisingly he grinned. 'Old habits die hard. Are we going to spend our evening arguing? I thought you might be feeling like company, but perhaps I was wrong. I'll go again, before I get kicked out.'

'No, wait.' She bit her lip; even his company would be better than none. 'I shouldn't have said that—I'm sorry.'

Strong brows rose in surprise. 'Apology accepted,' he said quietly. 'Would you like to join me?'

'I'll have gin, with plenty of lime in it, please.' She studied him as he poured her drink, the strong capable hands with their long tapering fingers, well looked after despite the fact that he worked hard for a living. She liked a man with well manicured nails. His grey shirt, a shade lighter than his trousers, was immaculate, fitting him perfectly, emphasising the breadth of shoulder without being too tight to spoil its shape.

There was an unconscious proud tilt to his well shaped head and his blond hair was neatly parted and combed. He had taken care with his appearance, and she wondered why.

When he handed her her drink their fingers touched for one abrasive second, startling Amie into a rapid withdrawal. She had not realised her hatred was so intense, that she would feel revulsion at his touch, and her eyes were wide and apprehensive as she backed away.

Oliver frowned. 'I won't beat about the bush, dear frightened lady, nor will I stay if I'm going to have this effect on you. I wondered whether you'd given any more thought to my offer.'

So that was why he had come; she ought to have known. 'I've not changed my mind,' she said abruptly, 'nor will I. You're wasting your time if that's all you want, but as Peta's probably prepared enough dinner for two you may as well stay.'

'A grudging invitation,' he remarked drily, 'and as I'm starving I'll take you up on it. Who knows, you might find yourself enjoying my company.'

It was on the tip of Amie's tongue to say she doubted it, but she refrained. After a week being alone his presence would be better than none.

Peta no longer applied spices to the food quite so generously, and having learned of Amie's disability she normally served meals that were easy to eat with a fork. Tonight, though, it was steak, done exactly as Amie liked it but in one piece that virtually covered her plate. How the hell am I to eat this? she asked herself, wondering whether Peta had done this deliberately so that she would feel embarrassed in front of Oliver.

She glanced at her companion, but he was intent on his own food and appeared not to notice her discomfiture. She tried to break a piece off with her fork, but it was impossible, then she attempted to cut it with her knife, but it slid across the plate. She had visions of it shooting across the table and ending up on Oliver's lap, so she gave that up. Each time she looked at him he was busy eating, but when she saw a smile hovering on the corners of his mouth she knew he was aware of her difficulty.

'You could offer to help!' she spat angrily.

'And you could try using your other hand,' he replied calmly, the smile gone, his blue eyes regarding her coolly.

As on the last occasion they had dined together she pushed away her plate. 'I might have known I'd get no sympathy from you!'

'None whatsoever,' he agreed smoothly, 'though I might agree to cut your meat if you ask me nicely.'

He was teasing her and she didn't like it. 'I'd rather starve than ask you to do anything!'

His shrug was brief and the next moment he was continuing his meal.

Amie was hungry and eyed her plate, wishing she had not been quite so hasty. It was a shame to waste such good food. Perhaps she could pick it up with her fingers and eat it that way? She would have done had she been on her own, it would not have been the first time. But with Oliver Maxwell sitting at her side she felt reluctant to resort to such primitive methods.

Suddenly he laughed. 'You remind me of Sam, a dog we had when I was a kid. He would sit and look at his dinner until my father gave the command to start eating. Your expression just now was exactly like his.'

'Thanks,' she retorted edgily. 'You're so generous with your compliments.'

Still smiling, he reached for her plate and began to cut the meat into bite-sized pieces. Amie watched him, wishing she had the guts to pick it up and slap it over his head—it was what he deserved—but right at this moment she thought more of the steak, and her stomach!

Silently he handed it back and she forked up the pieces, relishing the tender succulent meat dressed in a lightly spiced sauce of Peta's own concoction. The ice cream that followed was no problem and afterwards they took their coffee into the drawing room.

It was a gracious, stately room, with French period furniture and elegant carved tables. It was already dark and Oliver switched on the lamps and closed the windows against the inevitable night-flying insects. These were things that Amie should have done and she found herself resenting his familiarity yet again. He acted as though he were the owner of the house and she the guest!

She drew in her breath and sat down on the edge of a settee covered in exquisite tapestry. It looked beautiful, but was hard and uncomfortable, and she hoped he would not stay long.

'Peta tells me that you've hardly left the house since you arrived.' He joined her on the seat and she edged away, a vibration running through her as their eyes met. There was something in the silvery blue depths that disconcerted her. He disapproved of her, she knew that, he had made it perfectly clear that he thought she had treated her uncle shabbily, but it was not that, there was something else she could not quite figure out.

He was a sexually attractive man for all his ruthless veneer and she wondered whether he had anything like this in mind now. She set down her cup and saucer on a low table and stood up, realising what a vulnerable position she was in. 'I've not wanted to go anywhere,' she replied lightly, pretending to study one of the many pictures that adorned the walls.

'Can't you drive?' he asked abruptly, 'or does the crippled hand forbid that as well?'

She winced, glad he could not see her face. He enjoyed hurting her, but she would not give him the pleasure of knowing he had. 'I expect I could manage, if I really wanted to.'

'So—your uncle's car's in the garage. What's stopped you taking that out? Frightened of spending your money on petrol?'

How accurately he assessed her! She clenched her one good hand and closed her eyes tightly, counting to ten before turning to face him. 'There's nowhere I've wanted to go,' she lied. 'I've been quite happy here. It's early days yet.'

'I don't believe you,' he said softly, 'but I'll let you hold on to your pride just a little longer. How about coming out with me tomorrow? I'll call for you about nine, and we can spend the whole day seeing something of the island.'

His offer had taken the sting out of his first remark and Amie found herself agreeing, 'I'd like that,' but even as she spoke she despised herself for her weakness. She ought to have told him that she was perfectly capable of transporting herself around if she wanted to.

His flickering smile of triumph irritated her and if she could have retracted her acceptance without it seeming as though she was afraid of him she would have done.

'I thought you'd agree.' There was soft assurance in his voice.

'You're so damn sure of yourself!' Her eyes flashed as she crossed the room and bent down to pick up her coffee. 'I don't have to come, you know, I can just as easily do a sightseeing tour on my own.'

'But it's more fun in a twosome,' he suggested easily.

'It would be, if it was someone I liked,' she snapped. 'But I'm not sure that a day out with you could be termed fun. Exactly what was your reason for asking me?'

'I feel sorry for you,' he told her.

She did not believe him. 'Big deal,' she returned icily. 'If that's your only reason then I've changed my mind. I want pity from no one.'

'Okay,' he said, 'let's say I regard it as a duty to my friend Philippe. He would want me to do this, he's said often enough that if ever you came over he hoped we would be—good friends.'

Amie choked over her coffee and replaced the cup. 'As he's no longer here I see no point in your doing what he would want. You can back down, I won't be offended.'

Oliver rose and lazily stretched his arms. Again she was aware of his sensual virility and felt a quiver run through her just looking at his powerful body. 'I've already told my men that I'm having tomorrow off. I'll go now, let you get an early night. I'll be along about nine, so don't oversleep or I shall have no qualms about waking you myself.'

Nor would he, she thought, walking with him to the door.

'Goodnight, Amie,' he said softly in the open doorway, surprising her by lifting her chin with cool firm fingers and kissing her, his lips hard and prob-ing.

Before she could resist he had withdrawn and was striding briskly into the darkness. She stared after him, but he did not look back, and she raised her hand, touching her lips still tingling from the shock of his unexpected caress.

She would be lying to herself if she said she had found the experience unpleasant, there had been a sharp awareness, an unexpected reaction which had sent shockwaves through her body. Oliver had known exactly what he was doing, had probably calculated her reaction and was even now aware that she was standing here like an idiot, consciously wondering what had happened to her.

Angry with herself, she slammed the door and bolted it. Peta had told her there was no need, that there was no fear of intruders—but there was Oliver; he represented danger right at this moment, and just in case she overslept she intended taking every precaution.

As it happened she woke with the dawn at five o'clock, to a pink rosy morning heralding another hot blue day. It took some getting used to, this idyllic climate, after the predictable unpredicta-bility of English weather.

She showered and pulled on a pair of tight white jeans and after a moment's hesitation a sleeveless red and white striped top which dipped to a vee at both the back and the front. Beneath it she put on a bikini, also in white, just in case Oliver should decide to go swimming. She was not sure exactly what it was he had in mind, but guessed that he appreciated a girl being prepared, and although she had no particular wish to make him happy, it was no use going to the extreme and ensuring an uncomfortable day for the two of them.

Promptly at nine he arrived. Amie had slipped a thin cardigan over her tee-shirt, but outside the heat met them and she was glad to take it off. Oliver eyed her appraisingly and she could not help recalling that brief hard kiss last night. Trying to hide her confusion, she said brightly, 'Where are we going?'

'The choice is yours,' he replied lightly. 'We can motor right round the island in half a day, if you'd like that, or we could go into Curepipe or Port Louis and look at the shops, or we could find an isolated beach and spend the day swimming and sunning ourselves.' He paused expectantly. 'On the other hand, if you're feeling energetic we could go mountain climbing.'

'I think I'd like to see Port Louis,' she said, 'and then perhaps we could go swimming this afternoon. I've been told the lagoons here are out of this world.'

'True,' he nodded, 'especially in the eyes of a newcomer. I've been out here so long that I've become a bit blasé about it myself, but I've no doubt I shall enjoy seeing it all again through your eyes.'

He looked at her warmly and Amie felt her pulses race. She wished he had not the power to do this. She should be resenting him, not feeling that he could become a good friend.

She slid into his low-slung sports car and watched as he folded himself in beside her. He too wore jeans, thigh-hugging in pale beige, and an open mesh shirt in a matching brown through which she could see the powerful muscular chest with its scattering of fine hairs.

He felt her studying him and smiled, a heart-stopping smile that revealed slightly uneven white teeth, and there was a dimple in one cheek that she found irresistible. He reached across and stroked her hair. She stiffened, but he did not pull back, allowing his hand to slide down the slim column of her throat, to linger suggestively on the swell of her breasts. At that she did draw the line and dashed his hand away angrily. 'If your idea is to get me round to your side you're mistaken!' she snapped.

His eyes widened in mock surprise. 'Lady, you don't know me. If you did you'd realise I wasn't capable of such a thing.'

'Liar,' she returned, but there was a lightness to her tone which matched his. Perhaps it was not going to be such a bad day after all.

Port Louis was disappointing. It had a beautiful harbour and a glorious mountain background, but the town itself had been allowed to decay. It was smelly and grimy and not at all what Amie had expected for a busy seaport and capital. Even so she could not help being infected by the atmosphere. It teemed with pulsating life of all colours and creeds, with so many national costumes—saris, dhotis, fezes, tarbooshes—that Amie was agog with excitement.

On the architectural side there were pagodas and mosques, British colonial-style houses and French-type balconied houses, as well as numerous modern square dwellings.

They were jostled along narrow litter-strewn foot-paths and often had to leap out of the way of the endless stream of hooting taxis and cars that flooded through the network of streets. It was fun, and Amie enjoyed it much more than she had anticipated. Oliver took her to the Natural History Museum where she exclaimed aloud over the super display of shells and held her breath when he pointed out a giant terrestrial coconut-crab. 'Legend has it,' he said, 'that these crabs can climb palm trees and cut off the coconuts with their powerful claws. Then they climb back down and slice open the nuts to get at the white flesh.' He laughed at her wide-eyed disbelief. 'Actually what they do is gather the wind-falls and saw them open.'

'Not a pleasant fellow to meet,' she shuddered, and he smiled, draping his arm easily about her shoulders.

Most of the shops were run by Chinese or Indians who asked astonishingly high prices and then en-joyed the bartering that followed. Oliver proved expert at haggling and when Amie admired an ap-pliqué picture made from sugar cane the price he paid was less than half of what had originally been asked.

She was entranced by the Indian silks and cottons, dress lengths in a host of vivid colours and patterns, her artistic eye assessing and appraising, sometimes deciding that she could do better. Oliver watched her closely as she fingered delicate fabrics and she guessed that he knew what was running through her mind.

'One day,' he said softly, 'one day.'

A pity she did not have such faith herself. She

was convinced that she would never use her hand again, had resigned herself to this fact and could not see the point in trying to use it, even though Oliver had reiterated the doctor's opinion that it was only by determination and sheer guts on her part that she would ever get it to work again.

They had lunch in a Chinese restaurant and Amie tasted shark-fin soup and fried prawns with bamboo shoots, and Oliver didn't laugh when she sometimes had difficulty in picking up her food.

Afterwards they drove up the coast towards Tombeau Bay, through avenues of sugar cane, criss-crossed with dark rock hedges that were reminiscent of the Scottish Highlands, alongside streams and rivers, and the shoreline that alternated between black volcanic rock and sun-kissed golden sands.

Amie was entranced by the giant banyan trees with their branches that had taken root and looked vaguely like stalactites, and the enormous colourful flamboyants which lined the roadside and provided shade from the penetrating rays of the sun.

When Oliver pulled over the soft top she looked at him askance, but before she could ask the inevitable question she had the answer. Overhead sprinkers were irrigating the canefields, drenching everything and everyone who got in their path.

'I wouldn't mind getting wet,' she smiled, 'this heat's unbearable.'

'We'll go for a swim in a minute,' he said. 'There's a little beach near Trou aux Birches that I know you'll love.'

'Secluded?' she questioned caustically.

He nodded.

'I guessed as much. I think I'd prefer Trou aux Birches.'

'Safety in numbers, you mean?' The dimple was very much in evidence. 'I'm not going to rape you, if that's what you're worried about. I can do that in the house any time I want with less danger of us being disturbed.'

'That was the farthest thing from my mind,' she said primly, but it wasn't. This was what she was afraid of. Oliver had set himself out to be the perfect companion, and succeeded. There had been a gradual relaxing of her defences until she could think of no one else she would rather be with. He had spoilt it, though, with his reference to sex. Theirs had been a perfect platonic relationship this morning, and she had enjoyed it, and didn't want anything more—or so she told herself.

Since he had brought the subject up she could not help feeling an awareness of him as a potential lover, and her stomach churned at the thought of that lean powerful body next to hers, those well-shaped hands touching, caressing, and her mouth was suddenly dry.

His eyes narrowed at the sight of her parted lips, the tip of her tongue moistening the dryness, unconsciously provoking. He shot back the protective covering and pressed his foot viciously down on the accelerator. Amie was thrust back in her seat and wondered what she had done to cause this flurry of action.

The car ate up the miles and a few minutes later he stopped. The beach was tiny, secluded and breathtaking—palm-fringed with crystal-clear turquoise waters lapping the white sand. A tropical paradise, there was no other description for it.

Amie's eyes were over-bright as she turned to Oliver standing a few paces behind her. 'It's everything you said. I never knew there was anywhere quite so beautiful.'

'You won't find a lovelier place than Mauritius,' he replied confidently. 'They rave about Hawaii, but it's not a patch on this.'

'Nowhere could be,' she sighed. 'Can we swim now?'

He nodded. 'Race you in!' and almost before she could blink he had stripped off his shirt and pants and was heading towards the inviting blue waters. Her jeans and top landed on his and she was after him, laughing, shouting, feeling happier than she had in months.

The sea was like silk against her skin, cooling, caressing, a balm that soothed away troubles in an instant. She felt like a mermaid as she dived and surfaced, revelling in the safety of the reef-protected lagoon. Out here in the sun-warmed ocean she could forget her disability, it did not matter, she could swim or dive or float or do whatever she liked, it made no difference.

She followed Oliver out to the fringing coral, found herself swimming between brightly coloured damsel and butterfly fish, admiring the flower-like anemones.

Back on the shore they lay on the sand. In a matter of minutes they were dry and Oliver produced a bottle of lotion which he insisted on rubbing into her skin. His hands were gentle and although he performed the task clinically Amie could not help knowing that he got just as much pleasure out of it as she did.

They lay back, their eyes closed, but she was as aware of him as though she could see him. When after a few moments she opened her eyes she found him propped on one elbow watching her.

'You're not what I imagined,' he said, drawing a finger slowly across her forehead and down her slender nose.

'How do you mean?' she asked breathlessly. 'What did you think I'd be like?'

'Shrewd, out for what you could get. You're not like that at all, you're soft and warm——' his fingers touched her lips and they trembled, 'and responsive.'

She wanted to brush his hand away but couldn't. She was hypnotised by those silver-blue eyes watching her closely, judging her reaction.

'Does that surprise you?' she asked huskily, her body heat not entirely due to the warmth of the sun.

'Yes,' he admitted. 'I'm beginning to think that Philippe might have been right.'

She frowned, a tiny frown that creased her brow, marred her perfect beauty.

Oliver smoothed the frown away with gentle fingertips, then kissed the spot where it had been. 'Philippe said you and I would make a perfect couple. It was his ambition that we should meet, fall in love and get married. He regarded me as the son he never had and wanted to live to see my children growing up to take over the estate.'

Amie stilled, suspicion forming, chasing away the heady exhilaration that had begun to make itself felt. 'Since my uncle's no longer here, there's no need for you to carry out his wishes.'

He smiled warmly, convincingly. 'I'm not. I like you, Amie, despite my initial mistrust. I'm sorry if I didn't greet you very warmly in the beginning.'

She didn't want to believe him, something deep down inside told her he was lying, but when he lowered his mouth on hers and began a slow, sensual assault on her senses there was nothing she could do about it.

His lips moved with an expertise that could not be denied, evocative, tantalising, creating whirls of desire, so that constricting emotion built up in her throat.

She offered no resistance—she could not, she was completely at his mercy. No doubt the setting had a lot to do with it, she decided hazily, the sighing of the sea, the whispering of the palms. It was all conducive to love and romance—*and what was she doing letting him kiss her like this?*

Coming abruptly to her senses, she pushed him away, watching as he rolled back on the sand, apparently unperturbed, his mouth curved into a mocking smile. 'I meant what I said,' and his voice was deep and suggestive and set her pulses racing yet again.

'I've no doubt you did,' she replied hastily. 'I expect you're very good at telling a girl exactly what she means to you, I assume you've had plenty of practice.'

'What makes you think that?' he quipped lazily, reaching out and pulling her on top of him.

Contact was explosive. The feel of his sun-warmed skin against her own made her catch her breath and close her eyes before he could read in them the reaction he had aroused. 'You—you seem to know exactly what to do,' she managed at length.

'To get a girl going, you mean?'

The humour in his voice made her look at him quickly. She wanted to slap him, to knock that smile off his face, but her arms were imprisoned at her sides and as if to add emphasis to the fact that she could not escape his grip tightened.

She felt as though he was crushing her bones and winced. Immediately he relaxed, but he did not let her go, instead he wrapped his legs round hers and then slid his hands up her back to cup her nape, pulling her head down until their lips met in a kiss that ignited a fire within her.

This time she did not want him to stop. It was like no other kiss she had experienced, and she was not naïve, she had had plenty of boy-friends in London. But that was what they were—boys. Here was a man, a real man who knew exactly what to do to get a woman to respond.

She wriggled ecstatically on top of him, felt his passion growing and was both afraid and exalted at the same time.

When he pushed her gently away she felt more regret than relief and lay back with a sublime smile on her face, her body a raging torment of desire, but she had herself well under control. It was nice, she thought, that Oliver had not taken advantage of the situation; many men would have, and in the grip of these heady, exotic surroundings she would have been incapable of stopping him.

'Time we went home,' he said softly, and helped her to her feet, brushing away the white particles of talcum-soft sand that clung to her skin, making each stroke a caress so that her heart beat like a hammer within her breast.

She pulled on her jeans and he did up the zip because he knew it was awkward with one hand. Amie slipped on her top and combed her hair, then watched as Oliver got himself dressed.

His smile was kind and encompassing and he held her hand as they walked back to the car. Neither spoke during the journey, there was no need. In the few hours they had spent together a rapport had grown that was to Amie incredible, yet she could not deny that it had happened.

I think I love him, she told herself in something like awe. Could this be, after so brief an acquaintance, especially after such a disastrous beginning, or was she letting the romance of her surroundings mar her judgment? She didn't know, time alone would tell her that. All she knew was at this moment she was one of the happiest women alive.

Shangri-La was empty. Peta had gone, obviously presuming that they would not arrive back until late. 'I'd like to wash and change,' said Amie, and gave Oliver a sweet smile as she mounted the stairs.

When she came back down he had rustled up a meal and they sat at the white formica-topped table in the kitchen, talking quietly, nonsensically, as only lovers do.

Later they walked in the gardens, the heat of the sun having faded and the cooler night air a balm to their skin. Amie's dress was of soft apple green lawn and it brushed against Oliver's thighs as they walked side by side, clinging to the rougher denim of his jeans.

Sweet scents teased her nostrils, heady, intoxicating, until she felt almost drunk with happiness. As darkness fell a sliver of moon rode the sky, stars twinkled and looked down on them, watching, observing.

'Are you happy?' asked Oliver, and his voice was thick with emotion.

She nodded, unable to trust herself to speak. Everything was magic and she was frightened of shattering it, afraid that something might happen to spoil this new-found peace of mind.

When they tired of walking they went indoors and sat together on the hard settee, sipping white rum mixed with fresh coconut milk. A smooth drink that increased her headiness and made her a little careless of what she said and did.

'I'm tired,' after her second glass. 'I want to go to bed.' She stood up and twirled and held out her hand. 'Are you coming with me?'

He shook his head, silver eyes gleaming. 'A tempting offer, but no, you don't know what you're saying.'

'I do,' she protested. 'I'm not drunk, I'm in perfect control.'

He rose and joined her, putting his hands on her shoulders. 'In that case, dearest Amie, answer me one question.'

She entwined her arms behind his neck. 'Anything, dearest Oliver, anything!' and she looked at him with her beguiling green eyes.

'Are you ready to sell me Shangri-La?'

CHAPTER FOUR

AMIE stared at Oliver, wondering whether he could hear her happiness exploding. She could feel it herself, like a deep tearing inside her body that started in the pit of her stomach and reached out until it had ravaged every inch.

It took every ounce of will-power to stand there and look at him, her face drained of colour, her skin taut across her cheekbones. 'You swine, you hypocrite, you despicable bastard! I hate you, do you hear, I hate you, and I shall never leave here, never!'

'You're being unreasonable, Amie,' he said smoothly. 'You've everything to gain and nothing to lose. Why, with the money I'll pay you could afford to buy a smaller place if you like it here so much.'

'And why's Shangri-La so important to you?' she queried heatedly. 'Why can't you buy something else if it's a bigger house you're after?'

'I love this place,' came the calm, infuriating reply. 'I've spent so much time here that I——'

'——Regard it as your own,' she cut in angrily. 'Well, it's not, and never will be, not so long as I have anything to do with it! And don't try the smooth lover-boy tactics again, because they won't work. I won't be so soft a second time, believe me. I've learned my lesson today, good and proper!'

His smile was hard, nothing like the tender affectionate glances he had bestowed earlier. A muscle jerked in his jaw. 'There are other ways, Amie. One way or another I intend to own Shangri-La.'

'Over my dead body!' was her parting shot as he disappeared through the door, repeating it quietly to herself when he had gone. 'Over my dead body, Oliver Maxwell!'

She poured herself another drink and swallowed it quickly. What a fool she had been—why hadn't she guessed that he had some ulterior motive? He had made it so clear in the beginning that he did not want her here that she ought to have realised it had all been a ruse.

Her anger mounted the more she thought about it and she threw her empty glass at the fireplace, feeling a sense of satisfaction when it smashed into the hearth. She went upstairs, leaving the shattered pieces for Peta to clear up tomorrow.

She lay on top of the bed, hot and angry, and could not sleep. The grounds of Shangri-La boasted a swimming pool and on an impulse she ran downstairs and outside, pulling off her nightdress on the way, leaving it lying on the ground. Who cared? Who cared about anything any longer?

She dived into the pool, gasping at the icy water —she had not realised it would be so cold. But it was what she needed, and after a few exhausting lengths she felt better. Her rage subsided and she was left with a cold, calculating desire to get revenge on Oliver Maxwell.

She hauled herself out and ran back to the house,

picking up her nightdress on the way. She was halfway up the stairs, her naked body still wet and
gleaming, when a sound below made her turn.

'You!' she gasped. 'What the hell are you doing
here?'

For a few long seconds he did not speak, eyes
narrowed, staring, assessing, as though he had never
seen a nude woman before. Ineffectively Amie held
the thin nylon material in front of her.

'I said, what are you doing?'

'I came back to tell you to make sure to lock
your doors, not that I expect anyone to trouble you
here, but it's a wise precaution.'

'Are you trying to say you care what happens
to me?' Her green eyes flashed and she tried to
control her shivering. She was cold now, icy cold,
but she was not sure whether it was through the
water or because of this man's presence. He had a
nerve, coming in here like this! She did not believe this was the reason he had returned—he
couldn't possibly care that much. He would be
glad, she thought, if anything did happen to her,
then he would get his hands on the house just as
he wanted.

'I wouldn't like you to come to any harm.' He
mounted the steps and although instinct told her
to run she stood her ground. 'You're shivering,' he
observed tersely. 'Go and get some clothes on while
I make you a hot drink.'

'I can look after myself,' she replied coldly. 'I'm
waiting for you to go so that I can lock the door.
Isn't it fiends like yourself that you're warning me
against?'

His eyes narrowed. 'I ought to put you over my

knee for that—I'm strongly tempted, believe me.'
He caught her arm and for one second she thought
he was going to carry out his threat. She was about
to lunge at him when he turned her round and
pushed her up the stairs. 'Get dressed and don't
argue. I'll bring your drink up.'

He would too, she knew that, she would have
to beat him to it. She flung him one last venge-
ful glance before scurrying to her room. She turned
on the shower and stood for a few seconds beneath
the warming spray, a quick rub with the towel,
into a clean nightdress and cotton dressing gown,
and she was ready.

Pushing her feet into mules, she went downstairs,
joining him in the kitchen just as he was in the
act of picking up the tray. Two steaming cups stood
side by side and she picked one up, flashing him
a false smile, 'This one mine? Thank you,' and
sat down on one of the wooden chairs.

'You should be in bed,' he frowned. 'It's so easy
to catch a chill when you do stupid tricks like that.'

'If you weren't here, I would be,' she defended.
'It's all your fault.'

'Was it my fault that you went for a midnight
swim?'

Yes, she wanted to say, you did it to me, you
lighted fires inside me and then put them out with
one swift, cruel blow. You disappointed me, you
angered me, and it was all because of you that I
couldn't sleep.

'I was hot,' she said lamely. 'It had nothing to
do with you.'

'It's been hot other nights, have you been for
a swim then?'

She glared hostilely. 'What is this, a third degree? What the heck does it matter what I do? It's my own time, my own house, and my pool, I can do what I like without having to take this from you!'

He smiled briefly, as though satisfied by her answer.

Amie was furious. He always knew what was going on inside her mind. 'I hate you!' she stabbed. 'Hate with a capital H, and the sooner you realise that and keep out of my way the better!'

'Hate's akin to love!' Oliver spoke so softly that she wondered whether she had imagined it, but before she could comment he had spoken again. 'Be careful what you're saying, honey, you might need me. After all, I'm the only person you know on this island and if I wanted I could make your life very uncomfortable.'

'How?' she demanded, scowling at him over the rim of her cup.

'I could withdraw Peta's help, for one thing.' His brows rose as he awaited her reaction.

'I could manage without her. I'm used to looking after myself.'

'I also happen to know that you haven't yet paid for any of the groceries you've ordered. One whisper that you could have difficulty in paying and your supplies would be cut off.'

He frightened her, this big powerful man, but she tilted her chin and said coldly, 'I have enough money, your threats don't bother me.'

'For how long? I don't think you've realised yet exactly how much it costs to run this house. It needs painting—have you noticed how it's begun to flake? It's the heat, you know, it has to be done nearly every year. And the roof wants repairing, if we have any rain you'll be in trouble. Oh, and the insurance is ready for renewal, had you discovered that?'

He sipped his hot milk and watched her carefully.

Amie was horrified and distraught yet determined not to let him see it. She returned his gaze coolly, wondering how she could even have entertained the thought that she might be falling in love. He was arrogant, ruthless, certainly the most detestable man she had ever come across. He had charm, there was no doubt of that, when he chose to exert it, but he could also be a calculating enemy, and right at this moment she placed him in that category.

'Have you nothing to say?' he enquired at length, 'or have I upset you so much that you're tongue-tied?'

'Do you know,' she said, studying his face, observing the deep grooves that ran from nose to mouth, the furrows between his brows as though he had perpetual problems, 'you're the most despicable man I've ever met. You enjoy hitting below the belt. You would take great delight in seeing me on my knees, begging you to help.'

The dimple appeared for one fleeting moment. 'This is interesting. Do go on, let me hear what other conclusions you've drawn.'

She shook her head irritably. 'You're impossible! Why don't you just go and leave me to wallow in my own misery?'

Silvery eyes glinted. 'So you admit that you might have problems?'

'I've never denied them.'

'Merely chosen to ignore them?'

She shrugged. 'If you like. I see no point in worrying about something I can do nothing about.'

His chin shot up. 'But you can, that's the whole point.'

'Oh, yes, I can sell to you.' She crashed her cup down on the table so violently that its contents spilled. 'That's the whole idea of this exercise, isn't it? Worry her, make her realise that it's not all a bed of roses, pile on the agony, she'll soon be ready to come round to your way of thinking.' She swallowed angrily and scooping up her cup again finished the contents. 'Let me tell you, big man, I'm not such an easy nut to crack. I might look it, I might appear the soft weak little woman, but I'm not—I'm tough, and you don't frighten me, not one little bit.'

Oliver pushed back his chair, scraping the legs across the stone floor and setting Amie's teeth on edge. 'Point taken. Time alone will prove who's right. Goodnight, dear sweet lady. You can sheath your claws now, I'm going.'

Amie waited until she heard the front door close before moving. She felt worse than she had before her swim. Sleep was going to prove impossible tonight, that was for certain.

Suddenly she remembered seeing some sleeping pills in her uncle's bedroom. She had meant to throw them out, but had forgotten, and they could prove a blessing now. She swallowed one with some water, and then, after a moment's hesitation, another. Within a short space of time she was asleep.

She dreamt that there was an intruder in the house; she heard him mounting the stairs, step by step, then the heavy footsteps came along the landing, nearer and nearer. Outside her room they stopped, slowly the door opened and a blurred figure entered.

She was too scared to scream, too scared to do anything other than hide her head beneath the clothes. When a heavy hand touched her shoulder she began to struggle, fighting back with all her strength.

'Amie, it's me.'

Oliver's voice reached into her drugged mind, her dream became reality. She lifted heavy lids, wondering vaguely what he was doing here, before slipping once again into sleep.

He shook her again, more violently this time. 'Amie, wake up! Are you all right? Tell me what's the matter.'

'Of course I'm all right,' she slurred. 'I just want to sleep, that's all. Leave me alone.'

'Do you know what time it is?' Oliver insisted. 'It's past midday. Peta couldn't wake you and she fetched me. She thought you were dead.'

Awake now, though still feeling unusually lethargic, Amie demanded, 'And what did you do, jump for joy? Did you think you'd frightened me into committing suicide?'

'I must admit the thought did cross my mind,' he said stiffly, 'but contrary to what you may think, I was extremely concerned.'

'Am I supposed to believe that?'

'You can believe what you like,' he snorted. 'The point is, what's happened to you? Why are you still in bed at this time of day? Did you drink yourself into a stupor or something?'

'I had a couple of sleeping pills,' she said simply. 'Some I found in my uncle's bedroom.'

'God!' He shook his head in exasperation. 'Didn't you read the instructions? They're very strong. One is sufficient, but not on top of drink, and you'd had a considerable amount of white rum.'

'I'd forgotten,' replied Amie airily, 'but now that you've seen for yourself that I'm still alive and kicking you can get back to work. You had the day off yesterday, don't forget. What will your men be thinking?'

'As a matter of fact they want to meet you.' He sounded surprised. 'Curiosity, I suppose.'

'Are they too aware of Uncle Philippe's dearest wishes?' she asked acidly. 'Am I to be paraded as the future Mrs Maxwell, or is that not part of your plans? It could be one way of getting your hands on this house, or hadn't you thought of that?'

She heard a sound in the doorway and looking beyond Oliver saw Peta hovering, jealousy all too clear in her almond-shaped eyes.

Oliver too turned. 'Ah, Peta, make Amie some coffee, will you, strong and black with plenty of sugar.'

The Créole girl looked at Oliver painfully before disappearing to do his bidding. He sighed and turned back to the bed. 'The idea did occur to me, I must admit.'

'But you considered the price too high simply

to get your hands on Shangri-La?'

He sat down heavily on the edge. 'Are you pro-positioning me, young lady?'

'I'd see myself dead first!' she spat back.

'Yet the idea did cross your mind—I wonder why?' He looked amused and angry at the same time.

Amie felt uncomfortable. It was clear the idea of marrying her did not appeal to him, and she wondered what had made her say such a thing in the first place. 'Knowing the way your mind works,' she said defensively, 'I wouldn't have put it past you.'

'And I know that had I made such a suggestion you would have immediately turned me down.'

'Too true I would.' She yawned, the effects of the tablets not yet worn off, and closed her eyes.

Oliver was silent and she wondered what he was doing, but when she peeped at him through her eyelashes he was watching her thoughtfully and she closed her eyes again, for some reason afraid.

There was nothing he could do, not with Peta in the house, but she felt vulnerable lying there in bed with only a flimsy nightdress and a sheet for covering. He was, after all, a perfectly healthy male, with normal male instincts, and seeing her here like this it was not improbable that he might wish to take advantage.

But he didn't, and she should have known he wouldn't. He was not interested in her in that re-spect. Yesterday's advances had all been part of a plan—which had failed, and she was glad that it had.

What would have happened, for instance, if she

had agreed to sell, thinking perhaps that she herself was part of the bargain? She had been more than halfway towards falling in love with him. How humiliating it would have been to find that material possessions meant more to him!

Or perhaps it was Peta he intended making his bride; he had been keen enough to get her installed in the house in the first place. The girl herself had made no secret of the fact that she adored Oliver, and although he had shown no outward sign of affection, it could well be that there was something going on between them about which Amie knew nothing.

Not until she heard the dusky girl return did Amie open her eyes. Oliver rose and took the tray and Amie watched them closely for some sign that would reveal their true feelings. But he was as imperturbable as ever, seemingly oblivious to the slanting dark eyes which rested lovingly upon his face, and the way Peta's body apparently accidentally brushed against his as she swung round to leave the room.

Amie hauled herself up and took the cup from him, pulling a face as the thick sweet liquid slid down her throat.

'Drink it,' he ordered, 'or you'll be fit for nothing for the rest of the day.'

'There's nothing I want to do,' she husked. 'Why shouldn't I stay in bed?'

'Because you're coming to the factory with me. Since you're the cause of my being here we may as well make use of the fact and fit your visit in now.'

She was too tired to think clearly, too tired to

refuse, as she most probably would have done had she been in complete control of her senses. She felt drunk, deliciously, stupidly drunk. 'That will be nice,' she whispered, and because she was still weak the cup slipped out of her fingers, and hot coffee spilled on to the sheet, quickly soaking through until it touched her skin.

The pain woke her more effectively than anything else and quick as a flash Oliver threw back the sheets, heaving her off the bed and yanking off her nightdress all in one movement.

It was her thighs that had suffered, and already the skin was glowing red. Swearing beneath his breath, Oliver dragged her into the bathroom and soaking a flannel in cold water held it against the inflamed skin. Constantly he reapplied the flannel, each time moistening it in the water, questioning her as to whether the pain was easing.

But it was not the pain that bothered Amie, she was more aware of him nurturing her naked body, of his touch, of his close proximity, and of the feelings that were welling inside her.

Only an idiot would feel as she did, she knew that, especially after the way he had used her, but she couldn't help it. She wanted to hold him against her, she wanted to strip him too and feel his hard powerful body against her own as she had on the beach yesterday.

By the time he had finished she felt weak with emotion and clung to him unashamedly. Fortunately he misconstrued her reason and led her back to the bedroom, where he set her down gently on the edge of the bed.

What sort of a man was he, she wondered that

he could be immune to her? She trembled, and felt his concern. He lowered his head and brushed his lips against her cheek. 'I'll find you some clothes, you'll feel better in a minute.'

In a minute? In an hour? She would never feel better. She loved him; for better or worse she loved him. It was as clear as the foaming ocean out there, as clear as night is from day.

She had no control over her emotions and apparently no control over her body, for she let him dress her with no thought to resist. It was fortunate that he could not guess, that he put down her passivity to a state of shock.

He even brushed her hair, and when he had finished he kissed her mouth, one brief searing moment of passion before he held her from him and led her out of the room.

'I'm wondering,' he said, when they were downstairs, 'whether it's wise to take you out today after all. Perhaps we ought to leave it until another time?'

'No, I'd like to come,' she said decisively. She didn't want to be parted from him, not for one moment; she wanted to spend as much time as possible in his presence, without him guessing the real reason. 'I'd like to see how sugar is made.'

'We'll eat first, then,' he suggested wisely. 'I'll organise Peta to fix us some food.'

He left her sitting in the drawing room, and was gone so long that Amie began to wonder whether Peta was holding him up deliberately. She was tempted to go and see, but was afraid that she might catch them in a compromising situation, and that would make matters worse. So long as she could believe that Oliver had no real interest in the young native girl, then there was hope.

When he eventually returned she had closed her eyes again and immediately he was at her side, lean fingers touching her shoulder. 'Are you sure you're all right, Amie?'

She reached up and took his hand, clinging for one desperate second before realising that if she was not careful she would give herself away. She pulled herself up and then let him go, walking across to the window and staring out at the exotic gardens with their flaming tropical colours. 'I'm fine, still the effects of the tablets, I suppose.' Let him think that, it was the best way.

He pulled a bottle from his pocket and held it before her eyes. 'Just in case you decide to do the same thing again. These aren't for you, young lady. Your uncle was a sick man, he needed sleep to help him forget his pain.'

'I wish I'd met him,' she whispered.

Oliver's face hardened. 'So did he. Let's not discuss that, it's a sore point.'

He would not forgive her easily for what he thought was her neglect, she reflected. It would have been so easy to tell him that she had not known of Philippe Duval's existence before that staggering letter from her father, so why didn't she?

Was it because it would look as though she was begging him to like her? She would never do that. If ever he did change his opinion it had to be because it was what he wanted, not because of something she told him.

CHAPTER FIVE

On their journey to the sugar factory Oliver told Amie that sugar had been introduced into Mauritius in 1639, adding proudly, 'We are now among the most technically advanced sugar-producing countries in the world.'

And she hadn't even known where Mauritius was, she thought sadly. Everywhere they drove were fields of waving green cane, signs of the importance of this commodity for Mauritius's economy.

'We harvest in July,' he continued, 'July to November. These roads then are covered with sticks of cane that have fallen from the lorries, and everywhere is the sweet scent of sugar. You can smell it now, I know, but dring the harvest time it increases tenfold.'

Smoke stacks all over the island were signs of the vast number of sugar mills, and as they approached an impressive modern factory Amie felt proud to think that this had been her uncle's. For the first time she resented that he had left it to Oliver instead of her. He, after all, was no relation.

But, prodded her conscience, Oliver worked hard for your uncle, he deserves it. And deep down inside she knew that he too should have had the house. She was beginning to appreciate something of what he felt. After all, she was a complete stranger, a relative of whom Philippe Duval had spoken but never met, and so far as Oliver was concerned she could easily have come over to see him, or at the very least written, so why hadn't she?

Oliver must have been very close to her uncle, proving his worth time and time again, otherwise it was hardly likely he would have left him all this. Had he really cherished the hope that she and Oliver might get married? Had this been behind her strange inheritance?

Amie's thoughts were brought to an abrupt end as Oliver parked the car and led her inside the huge building, and soon she became fascinated by his explanations on how the sugar cane was turned into sugar.

The giant rollers which were used to squeeze the juice out of the cane initially were still and silent, but she got some idea of how the cane was fed into it, moving from one roller to another so that the maximum juice was extracted.

The next process was to purify the juice and he showed her a jar of original dark cloudy liquid. It was while he was explaining the purification process that they were interrupted by a good-looking man, grinning widely, eyeing Amie as though she was the best thing that had happened to him in a long time. '*Pardon*, Oliver, how about introducing me to your lady friend? Is this the one you were talking about?'

Amie was immediately attracted to the dark foreign-looking gentleman, with the delightful French accent. He was tall, reasonably good-looking, and about the friendliest character she had met so far on the island.

'Marcel?' Oliver did not sound very pleased. 'Trust you to be the first to try and make her acquaintance!'

'You've been holding out,' said the man called Marcel. 'You never said how pretty she was, a pure English rose, no less, with petal soft skin and beguiling green eyes.' He reached out and took her hand, kissing the back in an exaggerated Gallic gesture. 'Marcel Pitot at your service. I am Oliver's chief engineer.'

Amie smiled delightedly. 'Amie Douglas,' she responded readily.

'Amie? A name as sweet as yourself.' He pronounced it as though it were something special and Amie felt herself colouring.

Oliver frowned. 'Enough of the histrionics, Marcel. Please get back to work.'

The dark man shrugged nonchalantly. 'You're the boss, anything you say, but you haven't seen the last of me, Amie. What are you doing tonight? Any chance of you coming out with me for a meal?'

'She's dining with me,' said Oliver tightly.

'I seem to recall you saying she was not your type.' Marcel met his employer's eyes and there was a challenge in them that could not be disputed.

'Did I?' asked Oliver coldly. 'I don't remember, and the fact remains that Miss Douglas is dining with me tonight.'

'Don't I have any say in the matter?' asked Amie. This was a side to Oliver she did not like and despite all her new-found feelings she had no intention of allowing him to dictate to her. 'I too have no recollection of you asking me out. I should very much like to accept your invitation, Marcel. It will make quite a change to dine out with a *gentleman*.'

Oliver was furious and made no attempt to hide it. 'Young lady, you will do as I say. Marcel, back to work, I'll see you later.'

The other man strode easily away, but not before he said to Amie, 'Some other time, perhaps, *chérie*. You will be hearing from me.'

As soon as he was out of earshot Amie cried heatedly, 'You don't own me, Oliver Maxwell—you had no right to interfere!'

'I know Marcel,' he countered tightly. 'He's a lecherous villain and I forbid you to go out with him.'

'Forbid?' Amie was incredulous. 'You sound like my father. Is that how you see yourself—a sort of guardian figure who's compelled to look after his friend's niece because she's no money and no sense and precious little anything else that he wants—except a house?'

His face grim, Oliver caught her arm and yanked her round. 'Let's get the hell out of here before I do something I'll regret.'

'You mean something that would show you up in front of your men,' taunted Amie as she caught sight of several others coming in their direction.

The grip on her arm tightened and she almost cried out in pain. 'I couldn't care less what anyone thinks about me, it's you I want to save from embarrassment.'

'I doubt it,' she snapped, even as she felt herself hustled along. 'After all I've gone through with you nothing can embarrass me any more!'

His nostrils flared and his eyes glittered like diamonds as he pushed her mercilessly in front of him. Sliding into the car, she almost fell over her feet and fumed silently as she waited for him to get in beside her.

The short journey home was spiced with tension and Amie was confident that Oliver would follow her into the house, ensure that she didn't go out again that night. But he didn't, he dropped her off and drove away fast and furiously, a cloud of dust hiding the car from view within seconds.

For some idiotic reason she wondered what his house would be like. Whether he would bother to cook himself a meal, or whether his anger would be all the nourishment he required.

As her own temper subsided she thought about him more and more and realised that she had hardly been fair. It was natural that he knew what Marcel Pitot was like and she ought not to have gone against his wishes, saying that she wanted to dine with him.

The trouble was, Marcel had been so friendly, so completely opposite to her own first meeting with Oliver, that she could not help liking him. He would be good company, she was sure, and even though she loved Oliver it would be nice to go out with a man who would flatter her and make her feel deliciously feminine.

There was something of the romantic in Marcel that would appeal to any girl. If he should get in touch and ask her out again she would go—not to spite Oliver, but because she felt the need of other friends.

When the telephone rang an hour or so later she was startled. It hadn't worked before and Oliver had said nothing about getting it fixed. When she lifted the receiver she said breathlessly, 'Marcel, is that you?' For some reason she knew it was him and felt a quiver run through her at the thought of defying Oliver.

'Marcel?' Oliver's voice vibrated into her ear so loudly that she jumped. 'Has he been phoning you already?'

She shook her head, even though he couldn't see. 'No, Oliver. I—I just thought it—might be him.'

'Expecting him, were you?'

She had no need to see him to visualise the sneer on his face. 'I wasn't expecting anyone. I didn't even know the phone had been fixed—you never told me.'

'It was done today,' he said curtly, 'while we were out. I'm ringing to see if you're ready.'

'For what?' she snapped, puzzled. She could not remember making any arrangements. Indeed, when he had dropped her off she had had the feeling that it would be a long time before she saw him again.

'You're dining with me, remember?'

Oh, she remembered all right, but surely he hadn't meant it? 'I thought it was an excuse, to get rid of Marcel.'

'It was,' he replied tersely, 'but I never go back on my word. I'll be over in ten minutes, if you're not ready now, then hurry.'

Before she could speak again the phone went dead. She stood angrily holding the receiver for a few seconds before slamming it back down. If there had been a way of avoiding dining with him to-night she would have taken it, but she knew fatalis-tically that there was no way out.

It was less than ten minutes when she heard his car. He had not said where they were eating, nor given any idea of what she should wear. Just in case he took her somewhere nice she had slipped into a floaty chiffon evening gown, with long full sleeves and a plunging neckline. A slim gold chain was belted round her waist and she wore a gold pendant that had once belonged to her mother.

'Very elegant,' he said drily, after studying her for a few long moments.

'I trust it's suitable,' she said, when it became evident he was not going to tell her where they were going.

'Admirably.'

She was suspicious of his tone and suddenly rea-lised that Oliver himself was wearing only a pair of casual trousers and a crisp white shirt, nothing special. 'Where *are* we going?' she asked abruptly.

He smiled and took her elbow. 'You'll soon find out.'

His touch inflamed her, despite her antagonism, and she felt herself melting. As soon as they were outside she shrugged herself free. On no account must she give herself away. Their dining together tonight was purely accidental, a result of Marcel's invitation, not a gesture Oliver would have made otherwise, she was sure.

It was difficult lowering herself into his sports

car with the full folds of her skirt hampering her movements, and half afraid that it might get soiled on the floor of the vehicle, she pulled it up about her knees, holding it lightly so as not to crease the delicate fabric.

'Not the best of cars for evening dresses,' he said carelessly, 'perhaps I should have brought the company Rolls?'

Amie ignored his sarcasm. Quite clearly she was overdressed for whatever he had in mind, but she intended not to show it. Oliver would delight in humiliating her, she knew, and resolved there and then not to give him the chance.

Outside the gates Oliver took a virtually hidden track that ran almost parallel with the main road for several hundred yards and then branched off sharply through a forest of feathery casuarina. Dusk was falling rapidly, but as they emerged into a clearing fringed with palms and flaming crimson flamboyant trees Amie was able to make out a low white building, tiny, but with a charm all of its own.

She looked at Oliver expectantly. 'Your place?'

He nodded, stopping the car and helping her courteously to lift herself out.

'Why didn't you say?' she accused, half in anger and half in frustration. 'I would have worn something different.'

'You look delightful as you are,' he replied blandly. 'As Marcel said, like an English rose, dew-soft and untouched, a welcome distraction in these exotic surroundings.'

She didn't believe him, but followed across the small square of lawn on to the verandah that fronted the house. White-painted chairs and tables stood in readiness, gay with brightly coloured cushions, and bougainvillaea, oleander and frangipani grew in profusion against the sides. It held a magical, tropical splendour in complete antithesis to what Amie had expected. He had said he lived in a shack, this was anything but. It was enchanting, and although she hadn't yet seen inside she knew instinctively that it would be just as lovely.

'You look surprised,' he said, as he pushed open the door which was not locked.

'It's not much like your description,' she admitted. 'Did this belong to my uncle as well?'

He nodded. 'He has several houses dotted here and there. He was a very wealthy man.'

Yet he left me no money, she thought ironically. A vast house but no means of running it. Was there anything in what Oliver had said about the two of them getting together? Why else would he have done such a peculiar thing?

She wanted to say something, but knew that this was what Oliver expected. He was trying to get her going, he was on his high horse again about her never having been to see Philippe Duval.

'Oh, this is charming,' she said instead as they stepped into a room that was a living room and kitchen combined. Rush mats covered a boarded floor, the walls were white and simple, the furniture mainly cane apart from an oak dresser in the kitchen area. There was a washing machine and a fridge and a cooker upon which several pans were steaming and a delicious smell reached her nostrils.

'All mod cons, I see, how do you manage?'

'Bottled gas,' he replied. 'Your uncle insisted on his employees going short of nothing.'

'So I see. I'm surprised you want to move. You're very comfortable here.'

'It's all right for one, but I don't intend remaining a bachelor all my life.'

'I suppose not.' Some of her pleasure evaporated and she could not help wondering whether Peta was the woman he had in mind. Did the girl sleep here when she was not at Shangri-La? Seeing a door opposite, she pushed it open. 'Your bedroom, I presume?'

He let her go inside. There was a single bed, a chest and a small wardrobe, that was all, not much room for the two of them, unless—— She shrugged aside her thoughts and returned to the main room.

'Satisfied?' His grim smile told her that he knew exactly what she had been thinking.

'Perfectly,' she said lightly. 'Do you want any help with dinner?'

He shook his head. 'You're my guest. Go and sit on the verandah and I'll bring you a drink.'

She obeyed, sensing that he preferred to be master in his own kitchen, and also because she wanted to be alone with her thoughts. She was disturbed, there was no denying it. The thought that this could be his and Peta's love-nest left a nasty taste in her mouth.

She adjusted her chair so that she was half lying, half sitting, and then closed her eyes, listening to the soulful sighing of the casuarinas as a light breeze disturbed their delicate leaves, the ever-present chirruping of cicadas, and the occasional call of a bird before it settled down for the night. The air was full of a thousand different fragrances, and had the circumstances been different Amie would have been sublimely happy here in this tropical paradise.

The chink of glasses on the table interrupted her and she opened her eyes lazily. 'Still tired?' questioned Oliver as he dropped ice into the glasses and filled them with a pale green liquid.

'I'm enjoying my surroundings,' she negated. 'It's heavenly.'

He handed her her drink and dropped into a chair at her side. 'We can do a deal.'

She was instantly on the defensive. 'What, this for Shangri-La? No way. If that was your idea in bringing me here then you're going to be disappointed.'

'It was just a thought,' he said lightly, 'forget it.'

As if she could!—but, unwilling to spoil the evening, she pushed it to the back of her mind. She held up her glass, attempted to match his light tone. 'What shall we drink to?'

'To us?' he suggested, eyes mocking, 'that we might both attain our heart's desire?'

'I know what *you* want,' she said quickly, 'and there's no way that I'm going to drink to that.'

'Then let's drink to what you want. A pretty lady should always get her own way.'

She looked across suspiciously. 'Do you know what you're saying?'

'Of course. You want to keep Shangri-La, don't you, so here's hoping you do.' He swallowed a mouthful of the innocuous-looking liquid, watching her deeply through narrowed eyes.'

He was goading her and she was tempted to fling his words back in his face, until an imp of devilment took over and she smiled brightly. 'I'll certainly drink to that, Oliver Maxwell,' and she tipped up her glass.

Soon she was choking, fiery liquid burning her throat. 'What on earth's this?' she managed to cough. 'I thought it was lime.'

'My own recipe—don't you like it?' He was laughing.

'I like it, yes, but you might have warned me. Can I have some water to cool my throat?'

He had a jug waiting, evidently having guessed what was going to happen. He poured her a glass and then stood up. 'I'll leave you to it while I see to dinner.' Still smiling, he disappeared into the house.

Amie dabbed the tears from her eyes and sipped the satisfying water. The beast, he had done that on purpose! She had felt poised and confident, drinking to what he assumed was what she wanted most. Her only consolation was that he did not know what was really her heart's desire. She would give up Shangri-La for Oliver's love—not that she would ever have to, for if by some miracle it ever came about, they would both be able to live at the big house. But that was the depth of her feeling for him; she would give up everything to be able to hear him say, 'I love you, Amie.'

She was in control of herself when he called her, and to give credit where it was due, he had certainly done her proud. Oliver had not struck her as a romantic man, but the room was now lit by candlelight, the table perfectly laid, even if it was chunky earthenware dishes, and poinsettias floated in a bowl of water in the centre.

Soft music came from somewhere and he held back her chair, making sure she was comfortable before taking a seat opposite. 'What's all this in aid of?' she asked suspiciously.

'To make up for your disappointment in not dining out with Marcel, who would surely have taken you to the best place in Curepipe.'

Nowhere could be so perfect as this, she thought. Oliver's love was the only thing missing. She nodded appreciatively. 'I'm flattered, but you really needn't have gone to this trouble.'

'After you'd dressed up in all your finery? I couldn't let you down.'

And she didn't argue; she didn't want to spoil what could be one of the most enjoyable evenings she had spent so far. Determinedly she ignored the real reason she was here and chatted pleasantly as they ate their way through the several courses Oliver had prepared.

He had not been lying when he said he was an expert cook. They began their meal with millionaire's salad, or that was what he told her it was called—the heart of a palm, one whole tree sacrificed for this terminal shoot. Amie enjoyed the sweet, nutty flavour, but felt guilty at eating something which had been obtained at very great cost.

This was followed by crayfish in a piquant sauce, and then duck which he had thoughtfully cut into small pieces and arranged on a bed of rice and olives. To finish they had wild raspberries and ice cream, and the whole was washed down with chilled rosé wine.

Amie felt she could not have eaten better if he had taken her to the best restaurant in town, and her smile held genuine warmth when she thanked him. 'You don't need Peta,' she said, 'if you can cook like this,' and then immediately wished she hadn't brought the other girl's name into the conversation.

'Peta has other uses, besides cooking,' he replied, and there was a hint of suggestiveness in his tone which made Amie look across sharply.

'I'm quite sure she has—spare me the sordid details!'

He grinned. 'Jealousy becomes you. I love the way your eyes flash when you're angry.'

She tilted her chin. 'Why should you think I'm jealous of Peta? What you and she do is no concern of mine.'

'I know it isn't. Shall we take our coffee out on the verandah? Air-conditioning is the one refinement that this establishment lacks, and it's a trifle warm in here, don't you think?'

He was indicating that they were touching on a heated subject. Amie eyed him coldly. 'As you wish, Oliver Maxwell, anything you say.'

He set their two chairs close together and arranged the table conveniently beside her so that she could pick up her cup easily.

They sat in silence for several minutes, sipping their coffee, listening to the faint sounds of music which still played on inside the bungalow. She became fraught with tension, vitally aware of his nearness, of the aura of sensual virility that emanated from him. If she hadn't brought Peta into the conversation perhaps by now he might have——

Her thoughts were cruelly disrupted when he almost growled, 'Have you given any thought to exercising your hand?'

She had not realised he had been studying her, although she should have known that it was uppermost in his mind after the trouble he had taken to see that everything was arranged for her convenience.

'I see no point,' she replied indifferently, disappointedly; she wanted more from him than to sit here discussing her disability. 'I know I shall never be able to use it again, so why bother? It's a waste of time and effort.'

'A defeatist attitude,' he said brusquely. 'I've noticed how much more adept you're becoming with your left hand, but you'll never win like that.'

'Why should I want to?' she asked rudely.

'Because there's absolutely no reason why you should go through life with only one hand. You know yourself that it's difficult, almost everything you do requires two hands. If for no other reason think of your career—aren't you disappointed that you couldn't carry on with your course?'

She nodded. 'Naturally I am.'

He continued, 'I've seen the way you look at colours and textures and I've known exactly what you've been thinking. Have the doctors said that it's absolutely hopeless, your ever regaining even partial use?'

She hesitated, then shook her head. 'They reckon it's psychological.'

'There you are, then,' he pounced, and before she was aware of his intentions he had picked up her hand and taken the lifeless fingers into his.

It was fortunate she had no feeling, she decided, watching as he bent her fingers backwards and forwards, or she would be squirming on her chair by now, writhing in an agony of emotion. Even so her heartbeats quickened, drumming a tattoo inside her head. She became aware of something strong and vibrant flowing into her and before she began to take leave of her senses and wallow in the delirum evoked by his close proximity, she snatched away her hand. 'Leave it alone!' she snapped savagely.

He frowned. 'I want to help, Amie. I feel sure that——'

'Why?' she interjected acidly. 'Why should you want to help me—I'm your arch-enemy, had you forgotten? Or is it because I've got something you want? You're still trying to get round me, is that it?'

She was spoiling the evening, but she couldn't help it. Something inside drove her on, she wanted to hurt him as he was unwittingly hurting her by not returning her love. 'I might have known there was some ulterior motive in your asking me here, turning on the charm, making out you're enjoying my company, when all the time it's nothing more than another attempt at a softening-up process. You must take me for an idiot if you think I'll fall for your tricks a second time!'

Had she not been wearing a long dress she would have scrambled to her feet and run off into the darkness, but deciding such an exit would be undignified under the circumstances, she remained where she was, her green eyes flashing with a hatred that was at this precise moment very real.

Oliver stood up and pulled out a cheroot from a wooden box on the table, leaning against one of the verandah supports as he flicked open his lighter. Shadows flickered across his face and he did not speak again until it was satisfactorily alight, the red tip glowing vividly against the dark night sky behind him. 'I'm not fool enough to try the same thing twice,' he said tersely.

'Well, I can't believe it was Marcel's invitation alone that instigated all this, the soft lights and the music, perfect food and charming company—up until this moment.'

'What have I done wrong?' he asked innocently, too innocently, 'nothing that no friend wouldn't do under the circumstances.'

'Friend?' she shrieked. 'You're no friend of mine!'

'But I do have your interests at heart.'

'Only when they concern you,' she flung back. 'If there wasn't something devious behind all this why didn't you take me into Curepipe or somewhere? You yourself said that they have some marvellous restaurants.'

He leaned his head back against the post and pulled satisfyingly on his cheroot. 'I happen to enjoy my own cooking, and thought you would too— was I mistaken?'

What could she say but the truth? 'You know I found it excellent, that's not the point in question. Why this sudden interest in my hand, what concern is it of yours?' Even as she asked, the answer came to her. Why hadn't she thought of it a moment ago? 'Oh, I know,' she continued, 'it's just occurred to me. You are devious, Oliver Maxwell, much more than I gave you credit for.'

She saw his body tense, watched mesmerised as he stepped forward and leaned over her, his cigar stubbed out in the ashtray, his hands either side of her on the arms of the chair. 'Go on, Amie, go on.'

She thrilled at his nearness, drew in her breath sharply and closed her eyes. Suddenly she was afraid. Here were the two of them in the darkness of the night. If she angered him now what might happen?

'I'm waiting.' His voice held a hidden threat and she shuddered, her eyes abruptly opening wide.

'You don't intimidate me,' she said, her voice strangely confident considering the torment building up inside her. 'I'm quite willing to tell you, if you move away and give me room to breathe.'

'Not until you say what's on your mind.' His breath on her face smelled of smoke, but she didn't mind. She loved everything about this man. She loved the dear handsome face so close to hers, the shock of fair hair and the beautiful blue eyes which could be cruel or kind in the space of a second. They were cruel now, hard and remote. She had an insane urge to pull him down on top of her, see what he would do then, see whether he would still demand an answer or whether natural instincts would take over.

She wanted him desperately, with a primeval urge which she had never felt before. He brought out the wanton woman in her, and these wild, in-

credibly lovely surroundings did nothing to stem
the flow of passion. Only by holding herself taut
was she able to keep a rigid control on her feelings,
and she was glad that the darkness hid the colour
that suffused her cheeks.

'Your interest in my hand,' she whispered at
last, 'it's all part of the plan, isn't it? Get it working and I'll go back to London to continue my
course.' Her voice strengthened. 'Why didn't it
occur to me immediately? As I said, Oliver, you're
a very devious char——'

She got no further, for his mouth on hers effectively stemmed the flow of words. Instinctively she
began to struggle, yet all the time knowing that
she would give in in the end. This was what she
wanted, what she had been expecting all evening.
Adrenalin coursed through her veins and her lips
parted involuntarily beneath his urgent pressure.

Just as she felt every atom of fight drain from
her the phone rang. It was an incongruous sound
out there in the midle of nowhere and it startled
her, but she was even more surprised by the speed
with which Oliver moved. 'The factory,' he said,
'it's a direct line.'

A few seconds later he rejoined her. 'Trouble,' he
stated tersely. 'I must go—I haven't time to take
you home. Can you wait here until I get back?
I shouldn't be too long.'

She nodded. 'Or I could walk, it's not all that
far.'

'You're to stay,' he said flatly, 'and that's an
order.'

'Yes, sir,' she said pertly. 'Do you want me to

salute?' disappointment adding an edge to her words.

He looked at her closely. 'It's not funny, and I mean it. Stay put. Go to bed, if you like.'

A few seconds later he had gone. The drone of his car faded and she was alone. She switched on the lights and closed the door. She passed away the time by washing up, a slow laborious task she usually abhorred, but because she was doing it for Oliver she found herself enjoying it. That was love for you, she thought bitterly; it was making her soft.

When the room was tidy she settled down on one of the cane chairs with its curving arms and high cushioned back. She felt deliciously drowsy and wondered whether to take him up on his offer and go to bed. Could she trust him sufficiently to wake her and take her home when he came back?

Perhaps it didn't matter; a night spent with Oliver would be infinitely more enjoyable than one up at the big house on her own. She asked herself weakly what was happening to her moral values. Prior to falling in love with him nothing would have induced her to spend the night with a man.

She moved stiffly and decided that she might as well relax in comfort. The bed was soft and inviting. She slipped off her dress and crawled between the sheets.

Much later a sound disturbed her and she sensed rather than saw him in the room. 'Oliver,' she said dreamily, and held out her hand. 'I was waiting for you.'

She heard his swiftly indrawn breath and the

rustle of clothes as he hastily undressed. A quiver ran through her at the thought of what was in store and she felt one last moment of unease before allowing her love to race to the surface.

He was warm and hard in her arms, the sheets had been flung to the floor in his urgency, but it was not until his probing hands hurt and his hot mouth sought hers in a kiss that was repugnant and in no way as she remembered that she realised it was not Oliver.

She screamed and clawed and yelled. 'Let me go, you beast! Who the devil are you, bursting in here, pretending you're Oliver!'

'*Ma chérie.*' The harsh whisper told her all she wanted to know.

'Marcel!' She tried to scramble off the bed, but he held her down easily, laughing crudely and displaying none of the charm she had seen that afternoon.

'Oliver sent me to tell you that he has been delayed,' he said thickly, 'and what are friends for if they cannot help out? I must admit I didn't think he had gone this far, but as you were so obviously ready and willing I——'

'Oliver didn't send you,' she cut in hotly. 'He warned me against you, told me the type of man you are—and to think I didn't believe him! Do you know, if you'd asked me out again I fully intended to go. God, what a fool I would have been! Oliver was right, you're a lecher. Let me go this instant!'

But the Frenchman had no intention of throwing away what he clearly thought a fortuitous bit of luck. 'All in good time, Amie, all in good time.'

She was repulsed by his hot lips and breath on her face, the groping hands on her body, and twisted and turned agitatedly, trying to fight off his heavy weight. 'How did you know I was here?' she gasped, hoping to distract him by talking.

'Oliver was at the factory and you weren't at Shangri-La—I went there—so where else?'

'He'll be back in a minute.'

'Oh no, he won't. It will take longer than that to locate the breakdown.'

His confidence irritated her, made her think that he knew more than he cared to admit. 'You planned it!' she accused. 'This was your whole idea—get Oliver out of the way and have a good time with me.'

'He deserved it,' sneered the dark man. 'He had no intention of asking you out tonight, not until he heard me invite you. You're not his type, he told us so at the factory, do you know that? He said you held no appeal for him, that his only interest was in persuading you to sell the house.'

'I know,' she said tightly, sensing his amazement but wishing he hadn't confirmed her suspicions.

'Yet you were willing to go to bed with him? I'm surprised at you, Amie.'

She was surprised at herself, but that didn't give this man leave to continue where he thought Oliver had left off. 'At least he's a gentleman,' she spat fiercely. 'He would never force his attention where it wasn't wanted.'

'But you were ready for him,' he rasped. 'He had it made, so what's the difference? I'm more than willing to satisfy you.' His eager mouth sought hers yet again.

'You're insane!' Amie twisted her head desperately to one side, clawing and scratching at his back, feeling her nails draw blood, but he was either immune to the pain or too emotionally worked up to feel it. 'Let me go, you swine!'

As his mouth came down on hers yet again she sank her teeth into his lip, biting hard until she felt the salt taste of blood. Marcel swore violently and backed away, holding his hand to his mouth. 'You little bitch!' he roared.

She felt sick and rolled quickly off the bed, reaching the door before him and slamming it in his face. On the verandah he caught up with her, swinging her round violently into his arms and clumsily trying to tear off her lacy slip. She pushed against him with all her might and somehow knocked him off balance.

As she ran across the lawn and into the relative safety of the trees, she heard him calling, was aware of him lumbering after her. Fear helped her move swiftly in the darkness, hardly noticing the pain to her bare feet. She did not see the branch lying across her path and when she fell her voice rose into the air on a note of pure terror. This is it, she thought, there's no escaping him now. But even as this notion crossed her mind her head hit the bole of a tree and a velvety blackness enveloped her.

CHAPTER SIX

When Amie opened her eyes it was daylight, and she felt stiff and uncomfortable and had a splitting headache. She sat up half dazed and leaned back against a tree, holding her head and trying to recollect what had happened.

It came back with startling clarity. Marcel! He had tried to rape her! Where was he now? Had he grown scared when he saw her fall, perhaps returning to the factory, telling no one she was lying here in the forest? She could have been dead or dying for all he knew—unless he hadn't been able to find her? Perhaps he thought she had been hiding and had given up his search? But surely he must have heard her cry out?

It was all one great puzzle, and the more she thought about it the more her head ached. In the end she gave up and concentrated on pulling herself to her feet. As she made her slow, stumbling way back to Oliver's cabin she conjectured on why he too had not come in search of her, unless of course he had spent the whole night at the factory and was unaware that anything had happened.

This last theory proved to be right, for when she eventually limped back into his house there was no sign of him. Everything was exactly as it had been when she left—doors wide open, the bed rumpled and her dress lying across a chair.

She went into the tiny bathroom that led off the kitchen and wetting a towel held it against her head. In the mirror she saw a purple bruise livid against the pallor of her skin, wide haunted eyes and tangled hair. She sat down and cried.

At length she decided to return to Shangri-La. There she could soak in a hot bath and enjoy the comfort of her own bed. It was a long walk, much longer than it had seemed in the car, and her high-heeled sandals were not the best of footwear for such a trek. She kept her fingers mentally crossed that she would see no one on the main road, knowing she looked an incongruous figure in her white evening gown in the middle of the morning.

Somehow she made it, and did not know whether to be thankful or sorry that Peta was not around. She could think of nothing nicer right at this moment than being pampered and looked after.

The bathwater was like a balm and she soaked in its soothing warmth for a good half hour before climbing into bed. She swallowed a couple of aspirins and rubbed olive oil on the bruise like her mother had when she was a child.

For a long time she lay there, desperately tired but unable to sleep. Each time she closed her eyes visions of Marcel's gloating face floated before her. How could she ever have thought he was attractive? He was the most repelling man she had ever met, and it would be a long time before she forgot her ordeal. All she could be thankful for was that he had not accomplished what he set out to do.

Had Oliver not taken the sleeping tablets she

Join the hundreds of readers enjoying Mills & Boon's Reader Service

Take these free books and you will meet ten women who must face doubt, fear and disappointment before discovering lasting love and happiness. We are inviting you to share the moving stories of their sadness and their joy, and then decide for yourself whether you would like to read more. If you would, the Mills & Boon Reader Service allows you to receive the very latest Mills & Boon titles hot from the presses every month, delivered to your door, post and packing free. There are many other exclusive advantages, too:

★ No commitment. You receive books for only as long as you want.

★ No hidden extra charges. Postage and packing is completely free.

★ Friendly, personal attention from Reader Service Editor Susan Welland. Why not call her now on 01-689 6846 if you have any queries?

★ FREE monthly newsletter crammed with competitions, knitting patterns, recipes, bargain book offers, and exclusive special offers for you, your home and your friends.

THE TEN FREE BOOKS ARE OUR SPECIAL GIFT TO YOU. THEY ARE YOURS TO KEEP WITHOUT ANY OBLIGATION TO BUY FURTHER BOOKS.

You have nothing to lose — and a whole world of romance to gain. See how the Reader Service can help you to enjoy Mills & Boon even more by filling in and posting the coupon today.

Mills & Boon Reader Service, FREEPOST, P.O. Box 236, Croydon, Surrey CR9 9EL.

FREE BOOKS CERTIFICATE

To: **Mills & Boon Reader Service, FREEPOST, P.O. Box 236, Croydon, Surrey CR9 9EL.**

Please send me, FREE AND WITHOUT OBLIGATION, the ten latest Mills & Boon Romances and reserve a Reader Service Subscription for me. If I decide to subscribe I shall, from the beginning of the month following my free parcel of books, receive 10 new books each month for £7.50, post and packing free. If I decide not to subscribe, I shall write to you within 21 days. The free books are mine to keep in any case. I understand that I may cancel my subscription at any time simply by writing to you. I am over 18 years of age.

Name _____
(Please write in block capitals).
Address _____

_____

Town_____ County_____

3RIC

Postcode _____
Send no money. Take no risks.   No stamp needed.

A special offer for readers of Mills & Boon

Ten Mills & Boon Romances-FREE

We are offering you the chance to enjoy the ten very latest Mills & Boon Romances absolutely FREE and without obligation. This is your special introduction to the Mills & Boon Reader Service.

Allyne — THE CHALLENGE
Wibberley — MAN OF POWER
Field — THE WINDS OF W...
Thorpe — NO PASSING FAN...
Dailey — THE IVORY CAN...
Dailey — HEART OF STONE

Mills & Boon Romance
SEEN BY CANDLELIGHT
Anne Mather

Mills & Boon Romance
THE UNWILLING BRIDE
Violet Winspear

Mills & Boon Romance
THE MARRIAGE OF CAROLINE LINDSAY
Margaret Rome

Mills & Boon Romance
THE IVORY CANE
Janet Dailey

Mills & Boon Romance
THE SILK... BOND...
Flora Ki...

would have risked swallowing another one now. She felt sick and tired and very sorry for herself, and for the first time she wished she had never come to Mauritius.

Oliver's voice downstairs woke her, but she couldn't be bothered to answer; he would find her soon enough. When he walked into the room she looked at him through tear-misted eyes, expecting sympathy and concern.

'What the hell are you doing here?' he rasped harshly. 'I told you to stay.'

Amie closed her eyes, her body felt limp and heavy, and if she had had the energy she would have got up and hit him. 'I've been having a ball,' she said bitterly.

'So what do you think I've been doing?'

She looked wearily across at him. He was haggard and drawn, his eyes red-rimmed through lack of sleep. 'Looks like you've been up all night,' she commented. She didn't really care, not at this precise moment.

'That's right, and I expected you at home when I got back. For once I thought I would have my breakfast cooked for me and perhaps a little sympathy before I grabbed a few hours' sleep.'

She groaned and dragged the sheets over her head before he could see the pain his harsh words inflicted. 'There are plenty of beds here, take your pick. Just leave me alone—I'm tired too. Why did you bother to come?'

'Because I was worried about you,' he ground savagely.

'You sound it.' Her muffled voice was as angry as his. 'You could have phoned.'

'I tried, but there was no answer. Now I know why.'

'You don't know anything,' she murmured, not intending him to hear and shocked when the sheets were yanked from the bed.

'What don't I know?' he asked brusquely. 'What's been going on, what——' It was not until then that he saw her face properly. 'My God, what have you done to yourself? How did that happen?' He sat heavily on the edge of the bed, brushing back her dark hair with incredibly gentle fingers and scrutinising the glistening bruise. 'Tell me, Amie, was it an accident?'

A calculating gleam came into his eyes and she wondered whether he had some idea of what had happened, whether he suspected Marcel. For reasons that even she could not understand she said, 'I got fed up waiting, so I decided to come home. Unfortunately I fell, my high-heeled shoes caused it, and knocked my head against a tree. I've a bit of a head, that's all.'

'A bit of a head? I should think you've got the beauty of all headaches! Perhaps I ought to take you to hospital, make sure you've done no damage?'

'For Pete's sake don't fuss,' she cried crossly. 'Go and get some sleep, let's both sleep, and then perhaps we'll feel better.'

'Here?' One eyebrow quirked interrogatively as he patted the bed beside her.

'No!' She didn't want him to touch her, she wanted no one to touch her after last night. She felt—unclean somehow, despite the bath, as though Marcel had tainted her body permanently with his mauling hands.

Oliver frowned suspiciously and she had the un-
canny feeling that he guessed she was not telling
the truth. 'I'll use one of the other rooms,' he said
at length. 'I haven't the strength to drive back
home. Sorry I disturbed you.'

Amie slept only fitfully, her thoughts with Oliver.
He looked terrible—she had never seen him so
worried or tired before, his face was ashen, and in
a way it was all her fault. If she hadn't encouraged
Marcel in the first place he would never have
taken it into his head to plan a visit last night.

In the end, sick with worry, she threw back the
clothes and swung her feet over the edge of the
bed. Although she hadn't felt too bad lying down
her head swam now and she sat for a few minutes
regaining her senses. Eventually she managed to
get dressed, although her head throbbed each time
she moved it.

She was relieved when she found Peta in the
kitchen preparing her lunch. The girl did not look
very happy. 'What is Oliver doing in bed here?'
she asked abruptly.

Amie wanted to ask how she knew, but instead
she said, 'He's been at the factory all night. He
came to—to make sure I was all right, and I told
him to stay.' She felt reluctant somehow to tell the
other girl that she had been at Oliver's bungalow
yesterday evening. Jealousy, as she herself knew, was
not a nice thing, and the less Peta knew the better.

'Oh—you are hurt?' Peta eyed the bruise appre-
hensively. 'What happened?'

Amie shrugged and tried to smile. 'I fell against
a tree—silly, wasn't it?'

'Does it hurt?' asked Peta in a hushed voice. 'It looks very painful.'

Amie fingered the swelling lightly. 'Only if I touch it, but I have a headache. Be a dear and pour me some iced lime, I'll take some more tablets.'

She was swallowing down the aspirin when Oliver came into the kitchen. He still looked desperately worried and tired, but his eyes were less sore and he smiled weakly. 'Black coffee, Peta, gallons of it. How are you, Amie, does the head still hurt?'

'Not so much,' she lied. 'How about you, you haven't slept long.'

'Enough. I have to go back to the factory. We're losing money with the plant at a standstill. I can't understand why the centrifugals won't work.'

Amie thought she could, but hesitated to implicate Marcel without proof. 'What are centrifugals?' she asked.

'They're machines like big spin dryers, they separate the sugar crystals from the molasses.' Oliver spoke absently, his mind already back at the mill, a deep frown creasing his brow. 'I could almost swear that the machines have been tampered with, but why should anyone want to do that? It's a mystery.'

'Can I come with you?' asked Amie impulsively. She must speak to Marcel, make him realise that messing with Oliver's expensive equipment would get him nowhere. She had no thought for herself, that she might get involved in deeper trouble. It was Oliver who was important to her at this moment. It hurt her to see him worried like this.

'No.' He shook his head decisively. 'You're in no fit state to hang around. I could be hours.'

'Please,' she begged, switching her luminous green eyes to his. 'I can sit in your office. Perhaps I can even do some work for you, you never know.'

'Why?' He was suspicious. 'Why do you care about me all of a sudden?'

'No reason,' she said lightly. 'But I feel involved. After all, it was my uncle's factory, isn't that good enough?'

As she was so clearly determined he gave in. 'At least I'll know where you are and what you're doing, and we have a nurse on the premises in case you need her. In fact it might be a good idea to get her to take a look at you.'

She let him carry on making plans, all the time deciding what she would say to Marcel; and he was so tied up with his own burden that he did not notice how deep in thought she was.

At the factory Amie was compelled to go through a thorough examination by the nurse and then found herself in Oliver's office with strict instructions to rest. It was a busy, cluttered room with a battery of telephones and bulging files. Amie curled up in a deep leather armchair in one corner. She had not realised what an active man Oliver was, and judging by the way he was acting today he had not let the fact that he was now the owner of this place go to his head. He was working as hard as the next man—harder, most probably, because loss of production meant loss of profits.

The nurse popped in every few minutes to ensure she was all right—no doubt under Oliver's strict instructions, thought Amie drily. He was not going to risk her wandering off into the factory, maybe bumping into Marcel again. He had no idea she had seen him last night and that he was the sole reason for her being here now.

But as the morning progressed Amie began to wonder whether she would get the opportunity to seek out the Frenchman, and she was on the verge of defying orders to stay where she was, perhaps using the excuse that she was after the toilets if she should get caught wandering about on her own, when the man himself came into Oliver's office.

His good-looking face was flushed with anger, his lower lip where she had bitten it dark and slightly swollen. 'I've just heard that you are here.' He was breathing heavily, his dark eyes lewdly devouring her body. 'You're not going to get away with what you did last night, *mademoiselle*. I shall bide my time and I shall come again. You won't hide from me a second time.'

'Hide?' queried Amie. 'I was lying unconscious, in case you didn't know.' She pushed back her hair which she had combed forward over the multi-coloured bruise, and had the satisfaction of seeing Marcel's start of surprise.

But he showed no compunction. After a moment's hesitation he said, 'The fact remains that you haven't told Oliver. Why, I don't know, but——'

'To save your own skin,' she hissed viciously, 'though God knows why. But you're the reason I'm here now. I want to talk to you.'

For a fraction of a second his eyes lightened and he smiled importantly.

'Not in the way you think,' she flung hastily. 'I want you to go and tell Oliver what you've done to his machines, I want you to get them going again. He's losing a lot of money through you, do you know that?'

'I know,' he boasted. 'He can afford it.'

'You really don't care, do you?' She was shocked and showed it. 'You're enjoying seeing Oliver suffer. Why? What's he ever done to you?'

After a moment's deliberation he said slowly, 'He took my girl.'

Amie hid her surprise. 'And you're trying to retaliate? All I can say is that she couldn't have thought much of you in the first place if she allowed herself to be attracted by Oliver.'

'It was his money.' His eyes narrowed. 'She never looked at him twice until he inherited all this.'

'So where is she now?' queried Amie.

He shrugged. 'America, I believe. She was always talking about going there.'

'And yet you still hold it against Oliver?'

'He paid for her, didn't he?' he barked angrily. 'How else could she have managed it?'

'I don't know,' said Amie. 'The point is that Oliver's in trouble now and you're the only one who knows why. What are you going to do about it?'

He shoved his hands into his trouser pockets and leaned back lazily against the desk. 'Nothing—unless you promise to go out with me.'

Amie's eyes widened, pain shot through her head. 'You must be joking! After last night I never want to see you again.'

'But you're here now.'

'To plead for Oliver,' she said emotively. 'I've never seen him so distraught. He's worked all night, he only snatched a couple of hours' sleep. How could you do this to him?'

'My heart bleeds,' he drawled sarcastically. 'Make it worth my while and I might consider it.' He pulled something out of his pocket and held it in the palm of his hand. It was a piece of metal, so minute that it looked insignificant.

'Is that the cause of all the trouble?' she asked hotly, jumping to her feet and hurrying across to him.

He smiled gloatingly and closed his fingers, sliding his other arm about her waist and pulling her hard against him.

Revulsion threatened to choke her and ignoring the fact that her head felt alienated from her body she pummelled and struggled, did everything except cry out, because she didn't want anyone coming in here, not until she had managed to persuade him to get the machines going again.

'Quite a spitfire, aren't you?' Marcel muttered thickly, suddenly letting her go. 'Making love to you should be very exciting.'

'About as exciting as having your brains knocked out!' cried Amie, groping for a chair and sitting down. She felt ready to faint and it was only sheer determination that drove her on. 'Because that's what Oliver will do to you when I tell him what happened.'

'You won't,' he said confidently. 'If you had any intention you would have told him before.'

'You think so?' she scoffed. 'I'm warning you, Marcel, if you don't get those machines started right now I shall tell Oliver, and he'll kill you. I've gathered that he already hates your guts, so this might be the excuse he's been waiting for.'

'You love him,' accused Marcel abruptly. 'You'd do anything to save him all this upset.'

Why deny it? thought Amie tiredly, and nodded.

'Then agree to come out with me and I might consider it.'

Her head shot up. 'That's blackmail!'

'So what?' He sounded unconcerned. 'You want Oliver happy, you want the factory running smoothly again. An evening out with me is a small price to pay.'

Amie considered the alternative. Marcel was the chief engineer; he probably knew more about these machines than Oliver. It could be days before the trouble was discovered, Marcel would not be so stupid as to do something that would be found out immediately; he was too cunning, too devious by far to let himself get caught. And all the time Oliver would be pushing himself to the limit, forcing himself to work hour after hour after hour with only the very minimum of sleep. Could she do this to him?

'I could tell him you've sabotaged the machines,' she said slowly.

'He wouldn't believe you, especially since you've not told him about last night. When I was with you he thought I was at home in bed. It was his idea I snatch a few hours' sleep. "We'll take it in turns," he said, "until we locate the trouble. No sense us both wearing ourselves out." '

He was right, damn him. Oliver wouldn't believe her, not now. He might have, if she had told him straight away, and she wouldn't have liked to have been in Marcel's shoes then. But now, even if she did tell him, Marcel would deny it. By not giving him away she had inadvertently played right into his hands.

'If I did come out with you,' she said hesitantly, 'it would have to be somewhere where there were plenty of other people, and you would have to promise not to lay a finger on me.'

'Of course,' he said blithely. 'You have my word.'

For what it was, she thought uneasily. Marcel's word meant nothing. But if by doing this she could save Oliver heartache she was prepared to accede. She would just have to watch him like a hawk, make sure she got herself into no compromising circumstances.

'Very well,' she said quietly, 'but only if you get those machines going *now*.'

His smile was triumphant and, to use Oliver's own words, lecherous. But Amie tried to ignore this, ignore too the thumping of her heart when he kissed her hotly full on the lips. 'You'll be hearing from me, *chérie*.'

When he had gone she wiped her hand across the back of her mouth, disgusted with him and with herself. She felt sick and hastily swallowed the glass of water left by the nurse.

Half an hour later Oliver walked in, his face transformed. Though it was still lined with fatigue he was smiling.

'Are they working?' she asked huskily.

He nodded. 'Marcel did it. He's a good engineer. I dislike him as a man—but by jove, he knows what he's doing with those machines.'

'What was it?' she questioned innocently.

'Oh, nothing you'd understand, a little part that

had slipped out—something I never thought of checking, something that could only happen once in a hundred years. I still don't understand exactly how it happened, but right at this moment I don't care. All I want to do is go to bed—you too, by the look of it. You look ghastly. Are you sure you're all right?'

She nodded and walked with him from the room, grateful during the short journey home that he made no attempt to speak. He dropped her off at Shangri-La and went back to his own place, unconsciously echoing Marcel's parting words, 'You'll be hearing from me.'

For the next few days Amie was on tenterhooks, she stayed close to the house, afraid to go out in case she bumped into Marcel, and all the time waiting for the phone to ring, for the invitation to be issued. It was a date she had never felt less like keeping in her life, but she would not go back on her word, not when Oliver's whole livelihood was at stake.

She knew without a shadow of doubt that Marcel would not think twice about ruining Oliver if she let him down, and the longer he kept her waiting the more on edge she became. It did not help that Oliver too seemed to be keeping out of the way, and it hurt that he had not even bothered to enquire how she was.

When she questioned Peta all the information she got was that he was busy at the factory. But there was a light in the girl's eyes as she spoke, and Amie could not help wondering whether he was spending his spare time with her.

Each evening after dinner Peta disappeared, not

returning until the next morning when it was time
to prepare Amie's breakfast. She had never found
out whether the girl had a home and parents of
her own, so it was anyone's guess where she went.
Oliver's bungalow was the most likely place, in
Amie's opinion.

She could have rung Oliver, now that the phone
was working, but that would make it look as though
she needed him, and she had told him quite defi-
nitely on more than one occasion that she was quite
capable of running Shangri-La without any help
from him.

Sometimes, when she looked at the peeling paint
and checked on her dwindling bank balance, she
wondered exactly how much longer she could hold
out. It was stupid really, pretending to herself that
she was never going to give up Shangri-La, for one
day she would have to, and when that day came
Oliver Maxwell would take great delight in saying that he had told her so.

In the end she did phone him; she had no choice.
The air-conditioning wouldn't work, and even with
the windows open the house was like a furnace. It
would have been a simple matter to call in the pro-
fessionals, but that cost money. Oliver was capable
of pinpointing the trouble, she was sure.

She phoned him late one night, holding her
breath in case Peta answered and feeling relief flow
over her when his sonorous tones asked who was
calling.

'It's me,' she said faintly. 'I'm having trouble
with the air-conditioning. Do you think you could
come and take a look?' She had had to get it
out quickly before she backed down, and now, too

late, she realised how abrupt she had sounded.

She sensed him smiling, a cynical, confident smile, almost as if he had known that it would be she who contacted him first. 'Do you want me to come now?' and his voice was purposely sensual, vibrating with emotion that set Amie's nerves quivering.

'When—when you've got time,' she husked. 'There's no rush.'

'Except that you're feeling rather too warm and uncomfortable? Any particular reason why you've called me? I can give you the name of the firm who installed it, if you like. They might locate the trouble more quickly.'

'Oh, no, it doesn't matter,' she said hastily. 'I can't——' She paused. How could she admit that she hadn't the sort of money they would ask?

'You mean you expect me to do it for free?' he asked intuitively, following it up after a pause with, 'It could cost you in other ways, if you follow.'

'Like what?' she asked sharply. 'If it has anything to do with the house I'd rather——'

'Nothing like that,' he cut in. 'I mean I might like a few hours of your company. It's time I took a day or two off, I've been working practically round the clock of late.'

'Any particular reason?' she asked quickly, wondering whether Marcel had been up to any more of his tricks.

'None that comes to mind right now. I'll see you in the morning, then, Amie. Pleasant dreams!'

She was up early, even before Peta came, only too well aware of Oliver's knack of coming into her bedroom uninvited. She had coffee waiting

when he arrived, and a plate of bacon keeping
warm, guessing he would take advantage of coming over here to get out of cooking himself breakfast.

They were sitting together at the table in the
kitchen when Peta arrived. She glanced from one
to the other and did not look pleased. Perhaps,
thought Amie wickedly, she's wondering whether
he's spent the night here. She did not enlighten
her. At least it was clear that Peta had not been
with him, and this made her happy.

It took Oliver no more than a few minutes to
discover what was wrong with the air-conditioning.
'It's the motor,' he said. 'I could take it to pieces
to find out what's wrong, but it would pay you to
buy a new one. This one's been running virtually
non-stop for several years, it's probably worn itself
out.'

'How much do they cost?' Amie was worried but
tried not to show it.

'They're not cheap,' he said indifferently. 'We
can get one in Curepipe. We'll make a day of it.
Pack your bikini, just in case.'

She didn't dare argue; besides, she found herself looking forward with pleasurable anticipation
to the next few hours. She had not realised until
now exactly how much she had missed him, and
her heart ached with longing and love.

It was a pleasant drive and as they neared the
town itself Amie was enchanted with the high,
neatly-trimmed bamboo hedges. As they moved between the rows of green all was tranquillity and she
was entirely unprepared when they broke out into
the brisk atmosphere of Curepipe itself. It was a

mixture of old and new, of sombre grey business
premises and public buildings, and pretty glass-
fronted houses with gay curtains and well-tended
gardens.

Their shopping was soon completed and after
looking around the town Oliver drove her to what
he said was one of Curepipe's best known land-
marks, an extinct volcanic crater, Trou aux Cerfs.

It was certainly impressive in size, although the
cavity was now overgrown with grass, but what
entranced Amie most were the magnificent views.
Curepipe was perched on Mauritius's central pla-
teau and from this vantage point Oliver pointed
out the distant Black River mountains, what was
called the Toy Matterhorn, the Trois Mamelles
and Corps de Garde. In another direction was the
Moka mountain range with the peculiar Pieter
Both mountain, which looked for all the world
like a seal balancing a ball on its nose, and in yet
another direction the endless fields of cane. Nearer
at hand were the spires and rooftops of Curepipe
itself—and then suddenly, and to Amie's complete
amazement, it began to rain.

This was the first rain she had seen since coming
to the island, and she said as much to Oliver as
they ran back to the car. 'That's because you've
not been to Curepipe,' he laughed. 'It's five hundred and forty-nine metres above sea level and has
a more or less constant drizzle. If it's sun and blue
skies you want then keep to the coast and the low-
lands. You might not believe it, but in winter here
in Curepipe it's cold enough for lounge fires at
night.'

She found this hard to accept, but deferred that

he knew better. 'Shall we move on?' he asked, smiling. 'I get the impression you don't much like this.'

'It makes a refreshing change,' she admitted, 'but I prefer the sun. This reminds me too much of London.'

They drove to the east coast, more sparsely populated than the west where Port Louis was situated, but intoxicatingly beautiful. Oliver took her to Belle Mare, a long sandy beach which they had almost to themselves, and they stood looking out across the vast expanse of empty sea that gave the impression of going on and on to the end of the world. 'Can we swim?' she asked breathlessly, feeling the need to break the spell that bound her.

'Later. I'm going to take you to a tiny island a few kilometres further south. If you think this is beautiful wait until you see Touessrok!'

She smiled. 'It sounds dreamy.'

'It is dreamy. As you've probaly gathered, I'm not much of a romantic, but this place gets through to even a tough nut like me.'

Amie liked his description, it fitted him perfectly. Today was perfect. She had never thought when she phoned him last night that she would end up here like this. She slanted a glance at him as he concentrated on negotiating the narrow winding roads. The last time she had seen Oliver he had been tense and drawn, now he was relaxed and apparently content to be with her. His dimple was in evidence and there were tiny laughter creases at the corners of his eyes. He looked happy and she was pleased, and quite unconsciously she reached out and touched him. 'Thank you for bringing me out,' she whispered softly.

He took his hand from the wheel and put it on hers. 'The pleasure is all mine.' He sounded as though he meant it, but she knew differently. It was Shangri-La he was after, not her, and she would do well to remember it. Even so his touch aroused her, brought to the surface the wanton emotions she had tried so hard to forget these last few days.

She studied him openly now, loving every inch of that rugged handsome face, feeling an insane urge to run her fingers over the angular planes, to stroke his cheeks and feel the sculptured lines of his mouth. He drew her to him like a moth to a flame. Her heartbeats quickened painfully and she looked away, withdrawing her hand and resting it in her lap. That he was aware of her reaction she knew only too well, and cursed herself for revealing her feelings.

'We're almost there,' he said suddenly, and she came back to the present, staring with awe at the island that had loomed into view. He stopped the car and they got out, and Amie looked across at tiny Touessrok with its coconut palms. It was like everyone's idea of a desert island, and when a pirogue glided past it completed the picture and she was delighted.

'How do we get across?' she asked, hopping from one foot to the other. 'Do we swim?' It was not far, a stone's throw, no more.

'By boat,' he said, and led the way to where one was already waiting. It seemed to take the *passeur* no more than two heaves of his punt-pole before they were climbing out again.

There was a small hotel, a few tree-shaded bungalows, and that was all. It was a paradise, and

Amie wouldn't have minded being stranded on this island with Oliver for ever.

They had lunch on the hotel's balcony which was right on the water's edge, admiring the startlingly clear water striped in turquoise, aquamarine and green. Beyond the reef the colours changed to varying degrees of blue, from ultramarine to a very deep inky shade.

All too soon Oliver said they must go, and Amie sighed. 'It's the dreamiest place I've ever seen!'

'Is that why you've got stars in your eyes?' he asked. 'I've never seen them quite so shiny as they are now. Full of wonder, like a child who's been given a giant ice-cream.'

She grinned selfconsciously. 'After London this is paradise, something one only dreams about, or sees in films. Hobby said I would fall in love with Mauritius, but she didn't know how right she was.'

'Hobby?' he queried. 'Who's that?'

'My landlady. If it hadn't been for her I probably wouldn't have come. Apparently her husband came here before they were married, always promised to bring her, but they never quite managed it. Now he's dead.'

'So—why don't you ask her over for a holiday? She might even fancy staying on as your housekeeper. Peta won't be available for ever. One day she'll get married.'

To you? she thought bitterly, and cursed him for spoiling her day. 'I might do that,' she said brightly, trying to hide her sudden fall in spirits. 'As a matter of fact, for the last few days I've been toying with the idea of taking in a few holidaymakers. Hobby would be a big help. She's used to that sort of thing, she'd enjoy it, I know.'

'You mean turn Shangri-La into a hotel?' His face had changed dramatically, a frown thundered across his forehead and his silvery eyes glared coldly. 'Over my dead body! If you're thinking of that as a way to bring in money because you've suddenly realised you can't afford to keep going then forget it. I won't allow it!'

'*You* won't allow it?' Amie turned incredulous wide eyes on to his face. 'It has nothing to do with you. Shangri-La is mine, I can do what the hell I like with it.'

'So you can,' he said tersely, almost as though he had forgotten. 'But I shall do all in my power to stop you. Don't forget to take that into account when you're making your plans.'

'I won't,' she said sweetly. 'Thanks for telling me. You know what they say about being fore-warned.'

Oliver did not speak again on the journey home, his expression telling her that he was furious. She was sorry that their beautiful day had ended like this. She oughtn't to have told Oliver about her plans until she could present him with a *fait accompli*, but he had been so friendly, she had felt encouraged to confide. Now he was more against her than ever. She was upset, but determined not to show it, and even managed to hum softly to herself, hoping to give the impression that she couldn't care less what he thought.

He didn't even take her all the way home. He dropped her off at the gates, not answering when she said cheerfully, 'Goodbye, Oliver,' and it was not until she had almost reached the house that she remembered the new motor.

'Damn!' she exclaimed loudly, but resolved to suffer rather than get in touch with him again. If his conscience bothered him and he came to do it, okay, she would certainly not be too proud to say it didn't matter, but pride did prevent her from doing the asking.

She felt anything but happy when she pushed open the huge front door and went inside. What a day it had turned out to be! Thank goodness it was almost over. She went straight into the drawing room. A good strong drink was what she needed, something to revive her flagging spirits.

Her hand was on the bottle when a sound behind made her spin round. She had not noticed him standing silently by the window. Now her blood ran cold and her face drained of colour. 'Marcel, what are you doing here?'

CHAPTER SEVEN

EVEN as Amie asked the question she knew the answer, but she had not expected Marcel to call in person, she had anticipated a phone call first. What if Oliver had come back with her, as he would have done had they not argued? It did not bear thinking about.

Marcel came towards her, a sickening smile on

his damnably handsome face, and took the bottle, deliberately brushing his body against hers so that she shuddered and moved quickly away. 'I think you know why I am here,' he said thickly.

'It wasn't part of the deal,' she returned breathlessly. 'I said I'd go out with you, yes, but you have no right forcing your way in here like this—you could have phoned.'

'I did,' he smiled. 'Peta told me you were out with Oliver, something about fetching a new part for your air-conditioning. You were gone a long time. What kept you?'

'It's none of your business,' she snapped, perturbed to think that the dusky girl might tell Oliver that Marcel had been asking for her. 'Is Peta here now?'

He shook his head. 'She'd gone before I arrived. We're quite alone.'

'What if Oliver had come back in with me?' she questioned hotly.

'I was prepared for that,' he replied blandly. 'It was simple. I only had to say that there was trouble at the factory and I'd come to fetch him. How's he faring, by the way?'

Amie turned her head and refused to answer, gritting her teeth when she heard him laugh. It was not a pleasant sound, sinister, menacing somehow. He was determined to put an end to her relationship with Oliver. It was unfortunate he knew how she felt about him, but what he didn't know was that they had argued bitterly this afternoon, and as things looked at the moment it would be a long time before she saw Oliver again.

Marcel poured them both a drink and then sat

in an armchair, completely relaxed, very much in command of the situation. 'This is exceedingly pleasant,' he said smoothly. 'I wouldn't mind living here myself.'

'I expect you would,' she said drily, 'but don't think about it too much, because it's never likely to happen.'

'In fact,' he continued. 'I think we'll have dinner here. How does that strike you?'

'It doesn't,' she snapped. 'I'm not going back on my word, I'll keep my promise, but we're not staying here.'

'Any particular reason why?'

'Because Oliver will be here soon,' she lied. 'He's coming to fix the air-conditioning.'

Marcel looked at her steadily for a second or two, as though trying to make up his mind whether she was telling the truth. He must have believed her, for he said, 'Very well, we'll go out. Please get yourself changed, wear something sexy, I'm in the mood for an entertaining evening.'

'You promised you wouldn't touch me,' she snapped, suddenly frightened that she might be letting herself in for something that she couldn't handle.

'But that doesn't stop me looking,' he sneered, 'and you have a beautiful body, Amie, I'd like to see more.'

His insinuations made her go hot and cold and she almost ran from the room, half afraid that he might follow and supervise her himself. She closed her bedroom door and leaned back against it for a few minutes, feeling weak and sick and wishing with all her heart that there was some way she could get out of this situation. But for Oliver's sake she had to go through with it. Marcel would not hesitate to destroy him if she went back on her word now.

Still not sure that the Frenchman would not come up to her room, Amie wedged a chair beneath the door handle and then washed and changed as quickly as her one hand would allow. It took her much longer than it would have normally, haste making her fumble more than ever, but eventually she was ready.

Her mouth felt like sandpaper and her heart beat painfully in her breast when she at length made her way back downstairs. Marcel was pacing the room, turning swiftly when she made her entrance. 'I thought you'd run out on me,' he said narrowly, but his face changed when he looked at her. '*Ravissante.* You do me proud, Amie—thank you.'

She cringed as his eyes devoured every inch of her body, could almost feel his hands pawing her. In deference to his wishes she had put on a slinky, tight-fitting emerald green dress which matched her eyes. It had long sleeves, as usual, and a high neck, but cunning peephole cut-outs at the front which revealed the swell of her high breasts. Marcel seemed unable to take his eyes off it and she swung away in disgust. 'Let's go.'

His car was craftily parked at the back of the house. They walked round to it and he helped her in, and her flesh crawled as his hand touched her arm.

Just as they reached the gates Oliver's sports car screeched to a halt in front of them, effectively blocking their exit. This was the last thing Amie wanted and she slid down in her seat hoping he would not see her. At first he didn't, then he jumped out and came round to Marcel's side. 'You after me, Marcel?' he asked crisply. It was then that he saw Amie.

If she could have died that was the moment she would have chosen. Never before had she seen so much hatred on a man's face, and all she could do was look at him and smile limply.

'I hope you know what you're doing,' he grated, before swinging on his heel and walking back to his car. He lifted out the parcel they had brought back from Curepipe and flung it at her. 'If you're nice to him perhaps he'll do this for you as well.'

That was all. Marcel himself never said a word and Oliver reversed crazily away from them, swinging the car round in a screaming arc before racing back the way he had come.

Marcel laughed softly to himself as they continued their journey. 'Beautiful! Now he knows exactly what he's up against.'

'What do you mean?' queried Amie heatedly.

'He won't stop you coming out with me again.'

Her chin jerked up sharply. 'There won't be a second time, Marcel. One date, we said, and I meant it.'

'Oliver's fate is in your hands,' he said softly, insinuatingly. 'If you really love the fellow then you'll do as I ask.'

Oh, God, why hadn't she stuck up for herself in the first place? Why hadn't she told Oliver exactly what had happened? She wouldn't be in this mess now if she had. As it was she was completely at

Marcel's mercy, if he called she had to go running, unless she wanted to see Oliver a broken man.

The evening was as bad as she expected. Marcel took her to an exclusively intimate place where there was dancing after dinner, and he lost no opportunity to pull her into his arms.

She remained silent and withdrawn, but he did not appear to notice, deriving his sordid pleasure from the feel of her body beneath his possessive hands. She knew that he expected more before the evening was over, but was equally determined that he should not set foot inside Shangri-La again.

When he stopped his car outside her house she said tightly, 'Goodnight, Marcel. I consider my debts paid now, in full.'

'Aren't you going to ask me in?' He was already opening the door.

'No,' she snapped. 'I'm tired.'

'We could go to bed.'

'I thought you might suggest that, but it's not on—you've had your pound of flesh, Marcel.'

He frowned and while he was trying to puzzle out what she meant she scrambled out and raced up the steps. The phone was ringing inside the house, but by the time she had locked the door behind her it had stopped. She supposed it was Oliver, even though she could not really believe he would be concerned over her welfare after the way he had reacted earlier.

She peeped through a window and saw Marcel drive away. Surprisingly he had made no attempt to follow her in, something to be thankful for, although she knew that their relationship was by no means at an end. She had been foolish to believe that he would keep to his word. Promises meant nothing to men like him.

All night Amie lay awake, and by morning she had reached her decision. She must tell Oliver about Marcel, make a clean breast of it, and trust to luck that he would believe her.

She got up shortly after five, as soon as the sky had changed from pearly pink to a soft clear blue. Rather than phone him she decided to walk over, rehearsing on the way what she would say. But when she arrived at the bungalow it was empty. She walked all through it and there was no sign of Oliver. It was still barely six, she could not believe that he had already gone to the factory—unless there was trouble again. She picked up the phone, pressing the button which gave her a direct line. It was a long time before anyone answered and then she was told that Oliver had left the island. He had business to attend to in London and they did not know how long he would be away.

She was quite sure that this had been a sudden decision; he had said nothing yesterday. Had her going out with Marcel anything to do with it?

She felt tempted to stay there, savour the little bit of Oliver that still remained. His personality was stamped indelibly and she felt that even if she had not known it was his place she would have guessed. Everything was neat and orderly, ornaments displayed with almost regimental precision, but it was his books that gave him away—books on sugar, on every aspect of sugar growing and processing.

On the wall was a picture of the factory, and beside it one of an old mill which Amie presumed must have been when her uncle first started up in the sugar business. He had certainly come a long way since then, and it was strange her mother had never mentioned this wealthy brother.

Picking up one of the books, she was surprised to learn of the byproducts which also came from sugar. She had known about molasses, but had not realised that alcohol was produced for use in the making of rum, vinegar, perfumed spirits, and also for medicinal and industrial purposes.

She spent an hour looking through the books before reluctantly dragging herself away and walking slowly back to Shangri-La. Now that her plans had been thwarted she felt depressed and irritable, and laid all the blame on Marcel. Consequently she was far from happy when she found him yet again waiting for her at the house.

It was eight o'clock, the day had barely begun, even though she herself had been up for hours. 'What do you want?' she asked rudely, wondering whether Peta was about. It occurred to her that the Créole girl could be on Marcel's side, encouraging him to be friendly with Amie and thus leaving Oliver clear for her.

He smiled, his sinister smile, and Amie wondered how she could have ever thought it friendly. 'I discovered Oliver's left the island, and thought you might be feeling lonely.'

'I'm never lonely,' she spat. 'I like my own company—in fact I prefer it.'

'To a day out with an attentive member of the opposite sex?'

'If that's why you're here,' she blazed, 'you've wasted your time. Didn't I make myself clear last night?'

He inclined his head. 'Unfortunately, yes, but I'm not a man who takes no for an answer.'

'I'm beginning to realise that,' she said wearily, wishing she had never had the bad luck to encourage him in the first place. Even at this hour the heat in the house was unbearable, and she wiped away the perspiration from her brow.

'You're hot,' he remarked, and picked up a box from his side. 'What's it worth for me to fix this?'

The motor! The heat was oppressive and she desperately needed the air-conditioning mended, but at what cost? She certainly couldn't afford to get it done by an outsider, and with Oliver away for goodness knows how long, what other choice had she? In any case, even if she waited for Oliver, there was no saying that he would do it.

Trying to make her voice sound pleasant she said, 'If you're the friend you pretend to be you'll do it for nothing.'

'I don't do anything for nothing,' Marcel said insinuatingly. 'Come out with me afterwards and I'll have it working in no time.'

Amie sighed deeply. She was faced with no alternative, though after her resolution this morning to tell Oliver everything it was a particularly hard decision to make. If he had not left so hastily she would not be faced with this problem, and in some irrational way she decided it was all his fault.

'You'll come?' questioned Marcel impatiently.

She nodded.

He smirked. 'Good, I'll get on with it, and breakfast sounds like a good idea afterwards.'

She ground her teeth but said nothing. He had a nerve, this Frenchman. The more she saw of him

the more she disliked him. Once she had paid her
debts today she would lock herself in the house
and not move, not until Oliver came back. It was
the only way she was going to avoid Marcel; clearly
just telling him that she did not want to see him
again would make no difference.

True to his word, Marcel installed the new
motor in a remarkably short time. Amie had his
breakfast ready when he sought her out in the
kitchen—of Peta there was no sign, and she gained
the impression that the girl had left immediately
after letting Marcel into the house.

'Aren't you eating?' he asked, seeing only one
place set.

'I had mine earlier,' she lied, knowing that to
force down even one mouthful in front of this
despicable man would make her sick.

An idea occurred to her as she stood watching
him eat, and although she was not sure whether it
would work it cheered her up, and she even managed to make pleasant conversation.

'Where were you thinking of going?' she asked,
with pretended interest.

'I thought we might go out in my yacht,' he said
idly.

She was surprised, and showed it.

'It's nothing fantastic,' he continued, 'but if
you've never been yachting you'll enjoy it.'

Amie was tempted, and had it been anyone else
other than Marcel who was making the offer she
would have been really excited. But knowing that
he was not to be trusted she felt it best to adhere
to the plan already formulated in her mind.

As soon as he had finished eating he announced

himself ready to go. She smiled tightly and they walked together towards the front door. Her plan now all depended on him going out first. The trouble was, even though he was an undesirable character, he was a gentleman and stood back for her to precede him.

She wanted to scream and racked her brains quickly for some excuse to stay behind. 'Oh, I think I've got something in my shoe,' she said, dropping to one knee and pulling off her plimsoll. Marcel waited patiently, but still made no attempt to step outside the house, and she wondered whether he had guessed what was running through her mind.

Once her shoe was back in position she had no excuse, and short of pushing him out in front of her there seemed little she could do—and then, miraculously, just as they were descending the steps, she heard the telephone ringing.

Her reaction was like lightning. 'I must answer it,' she said, and twisting round sharply rushed back up the steps and pushed open the door, for once grateful that no one here bothered to lock them. Marcel had started to follow, but more slowly, and she was able to swing the door shut in his face, reaching up and sliding the heavy bolt across.

She heard him shout angrily and, weak with relief, she leaned back against the door, sliding down until she was sitting on the floor. The phone rang on and on, but she scarcely heard it, only Marcel's loud, furious voice and heavy fists banging on the door reaching her weary brain.

Her only fear was that he might try and force his way through one of the windows. They were all fastened, she knew, the only one that had been open was the kitchen, and she had closed that before they left. But if he took it into his head to break in, he could easily smash the glass. All she could do was hope that he would not go that far.

When at length all was silent she dragged herself up, not until then realising exactly how much it had taken out of her. Her legs would hardly carry her weight and she held on to the wall as she forced her way into the drawing room from where she could see his car in front of the house.

He was just climbing into it, his face suffused with dark angry colour. She had made an enemy, a dangerous enemy, and it would be woe betide her if their paths ever met again.

Even when the car was out of sight she could not rest, but paced from room to room distractedly, nerves totally destroyed. It was ages before she even thought about the phone, and then she wondered who had been calling. Was it Oliver, phoning long-distance, drawing his own conclusions when it went yet again unanswered? He would presume she had spent the night with Marcel, that she was with him still; he would have no idea of the emotional upset she had gone through.

And when he did come home he would take some convincing that there was nothing between her and the Frenchman, more than likely scoff at the idea of his blackmailing her. If only she had told him about that first night when Marcel had broken into his bungalow! It all seemed a long time ago now and she doubted whether he would believe her. He would want to know why she had kept it to herself in the first place, and the trouble was she did not really know the answer.

When the shrill insistent ring of the telephone broke yet again into the silence of the house she ran and snatched up the receiver. 'Ol——'

Her words died on her lips as a savage voice let forth a stream of angry French words. She knew that Marcel was calling her all the names he could think of and slammed down the phone.

When it rang again a few seconds later she said, 'Listen, Marcel, leave me alone, will you. I want nothing more to do with you, *ever*, and I mean it!' Once again she banged down the receiver.

She lifted it again after a few seconds, made sure they were not still connected, and then left it lying on the table. It meant no one else could ring her either, but who was there to call besides Oliver, and it was doubtful he would contact her again; he had already decided what was happening.

The tension of the morning had sapped all her energy, and it suddenly occurred to her that she had eaten nothing since dinner with Marcel last night. She went into the kitchen and toasted a slice of bread. After eating that and drinking a cup of strong black coffee she felt better, and going into her uncle's study she sat down to write a letter to Hobby.

Whether she went through with her plans to turn Shangri-La into a hotel or not it would be good to have the woman here. She desperately needed company, someone sympathetic, someone who would appreciate what she was going through, and Hobby was perfect.

She also wrote a brief note to her father, but kept this purposely light and cheerful, telling him nothing of the situation in which she had found herself.

She would ask Peta to post the letters. She could
not go out and risk bumping into the obnoxious
Marcel once again.

It was several days before she had a reply from
Hobby and during that time she had never felt so
lonely or depressed in her life. The older woman's
letter, though, cheered her enormously. She said
she would love to come, that she had been hoping
for just such an invitation ever since Amie had left,
and that she would be over on the first available
plane.

When Amie told Peta that she had a friend coming out from England to help with the housework
she had thought the girl would be upset. On the
contrary, Peta had looked pleased, but there had
been malice in her pleasure when she said, 'In
that case I'll go now. You can cope until your friend
comes, I am sure.' She had gone there and then and
Amie had not really cared. She had all day and
every day to do the housework.

A few days later, without warning, Mrs Hobbs
arrived. Amie was sitting in the window when the
taxi drew up, and as soon as she saw the familiar
figure she leapt out of her chair and was at the
front door before the woman had even begun to
mount the steps.

'Oh, Hobby, Hobby,' cried Amie, throwing herself
into her friend's arms. 'I'm so glad you've come!'

'Tears?' questioned the older woman. 'What's all
this?'

Amie did not realise that she was crying. 'I'm
so happy you're here,' she sniffed. 'You've no idea
how lonely I've been!'

Hobby's arm was comfortingly about her as they

walked back into the house. 'I could do with a cup of tea,' she said. 'What a journey—and then you can tell me all about what's been happening.' Her bright eyes darted about her as Amie led the way into the kitchen. 'It's some place, this, big enough for a hotel, if you ask me, and you're living here alone? Do you have any help with the housework?'

'Up until a few days ago,' agreed Amie. 'A girl used to come in, but we didn't get on very well. As soon as I told her you were coming she announced that she wasn't going to help any more.'

Hobby said nothing, but before Amie could make a move she busied herself making tea while Amie reached out a tin of cakes Peta had cooked the day before she left. It was cosy, having Hobby here like this, it reminded her of their mornings in the flat; unfortunately it reminded her too of the accident and the reason that she had come out here in the first place.

'I still can't use my hand,' she said, before Mrs Hobbs herself could bring up the subject.

'So I've noticed,' said the woman drily. 'Have you tried?'

Don't you start, thought Amie, but she said, 'Occasionally. It's no good, though.'

'So you sit around all day moping. It's no wonder you're fed up! Are there no people of your own age with whom you can make friends?'

Amie shook her head. 'It's a trifle isolated here, in case you hadn't noticed.

'But surely you've had the opportunity to meet some people? You can't tell me that you've been here all these weeks and met no one.'

'There's Oliver,' shrugged Amie, 'he now owns

my uncle's estate, and Marcel, his chief engineer, and then Peta, the Créole girl who used to come in every day—apart from them, no one.'

'I suspect you've not tried,' said Hobby, sipping her tea and watching the younger girl carefully. 'How are you managing for money, it must take an awful lot to keep a place this size going?'

'That's another problem,' said Amie ruefully. 'I've almost run out. I don't know what I shall do when I've none left at all. Oliver wants to buy the place, but I shall never sell to him, never!'

Hobby looked at her closely, her dark round eyes bright and shrewd. 'Why? Does the house mean so much to you, or is it the man himself you object to?'

'It's him,' cried Amie passionately. 'He inherited my uncle's estate and he wants Shangri-La as well, but he shall never have it, not so long as I'm here to fight him.'

Her old landlady finished her tea. 'Then you'll have to find a job, Amie. Money doesn't grow on trees, you know, you won't get rich just by sitting here thinking about it.'

'How can I?' asked Amie crossly, holding out her right hand and staring at it, 'with *this*?'

Hobby sniffed impatiently. 'You're a martyr, Amie, and you know it. If you tried hard enough you could use that hand, you've just got some stupid notion into your head that you can't and that's it—you won't even try.'

Amie felt the tears begin again. 'I didn't invite you here so I could be lectured!'

The woman was immediately contrite. 'I know, love, and I'm sorry, but someone needs to do some straight talking.' She was silent for a moment, then she said brightly, 'Why don't you turn this place into a hotel? Like I said, it's big enough for one. I'd love helping, it would suit me down to a turn.'

'Oliver won't let me,' said Amie, hating to dash the other woman's hopes almost before she had got going. 'I'd already thought about it, but he said that if I dared do such a thing he would fight me every inch of the way.'

'It's nothing to do with him,' said Hobby indignantly. 'He doesn't own the place.'

'But he likes to think he does. Wait till you meet him, Hobby, you'll see what I mean.'

'Then we'll have to work on him,' said Mrs Hobbs mischievously. 'If he's like most men he won't be able to withstand the pressure of two women for very long.'

'You don't know Oliver,' said Amie tightly. 'He's not like other men, he's a law unto himself.'

Hobby smiled. 'He sounds interesting. When am I going to meet this—wonder man?'

Amie shrugged. 'That's anyone's guess. He's in London at the moment, I've no idea when he'll be back.'

Hobby nodded. 'Then there's nothing to stop us making a few enquiries, putting out the feelers, so to speak; the more ammunition we have the better. Who knows, if we get things moving before he returns he might decide not to do anything about it.'

'*Might* being the operative word,' said Amie drily. 'You're forgetting that I know him better than you.'

'Are you in love with him?' asked Hobby suddenly, surprisingly.

Amie avoided looking at her companion. 'How did you guess?' feeling a warmth course through her just at the thought of Oliver in the role of a lover.

'The way you go on about him! There has to be something for him to have made such an impression.'

'I both love and hate him,' said Amie vehemently, 'though I don't expect you to understand that, not until you see him, then perhaps you will.'

After they had finished their tea and cakes Hobby said, 'Do you mind if I snatch a few hours' sleep? I'm totally exhausted after that long journey. My Fred never said anything about the time it takes to get here. Mind you, he was right about Mauritius. I've never seen anything so pretty, quite takes your breath away, doesn't it? Thank you for inviting me, love.'

While Hobby was asleep Amie prepared their dinner, and as she worked she thought over the woman's suggestion that they begin to make plans to turn Shangri-La into a hotel. The more she thought about it the more enthusiastic she became. Perhaps Oliver wouldn't do anything, once he saw how determined they were.

The house itself would need no alteration. Most of the bedrooms had their own private bathrooms, or failing that a vanity unit, and there was absolutely loads of bedlinen and towels. They might need more china and cooking pans, but otherwise everything was perfect. They could manage on their own to start with and then when things got going they could get a couple of girls in to help.

Already Amie could see the place full of people. Shangri-La—the name was perfect, a peaceful untroubled place where one could escape. Oh, she hoped they could go through with it, she really did.

It was over breakfast the next morning that Hobby told Amie about her visitor. 'It quite slipped my mind yesterday,' she said. 'This man came to see me just before I came away, said he was Ginny's brother. I didn't know she had a brother, did you?'

Amie shook her head. 'What did he want?'

'Apparently he didn't know about the accident, and he turned up expecting to see her. It was a terrible shock to him, he went sort of white and faint, and I gave him a glass of Fred's whisky.'

Amie felt distressed. After all, she had been the one who had been driving, so if anyone had been the cause of Ginny's death, it was herself. 'Did— he say anything about me?' she asked huskily.

Hobby shrugged. 'I gave him the details, I told him that you'd been injured too. I also told him that Ginny had said she was an orphan, that we'd no idea she had a brother or we'd have tried to get in touch.'

'And what did he say?'

'That he'd run away to sea, or something, when their parents died, rather than be put into a home. Ginny was only a baby, so she wouldn't remember him. He'd been trying to trace her for years, apparently.'

'I wish he'd never bothered,' said Amie, guilt making her feel quite ill once again.

'Now you mustn't think like that,' remonstrated

Hobby. 'It wasn't your fault, and you'd be as well to remember it. I told him exactly what happened, he doesn't blame you at all, I'm sure.'

But she did not sound entirely convinced and Amie asked, 'What was he like?'

'Nothing like Ginny, that's a fact. Charming on the exterior but as hard as nails underneath. One strange thing about him, though. Ginny's surname was Jones, wasn't it? Yet her brother said his name was Maxwell—Oliver Maxwell.'

CHAPTER EIGHT

AMIE felt as though she had been struck a blow, slumping back into her seat and staring at Hobby, her green eyes wide and shocked, her face distressed and drained of colour.

'What's the matter, love, what have I said?' asked Mrs Hobbs in concern. 'Do you know this Oliver Maxwell?'

Amie nodded shakily. 'It's him—the man who's inherited my uncle's estate.' She had not thought that matters could get worse between Oliver and herself, had never imagined anything so cruel as this happening. How could she face him now, what could she say?

'I see,' said the older woman, 'but you needn't worry, he doesn't know it was you. I gave him no names.'

'He'll put two and two together when he sees you here—he knows I used to lodge with you.'

'So what?' Hobby shook her head impatiently. 'He can't blame you, it was no one's fault. It was a bad night, there's always accidents when the roads are slippery.'

Amie's head dropped forward on her chest. 'Oh, God, Hobby, I love him so desperately, what am I going to do? I'm already blackened in his books, I was hoping to get matters sorted out when he came back, but now there's no chance, is there?' Her voice rose hysterically. 'What man would ever want to marry his sister's killer?'

'Now, now.' Hobby's arm came about her shoulders, her voice soothing and compassionate. 'Nothing's ever so bad as it seems, things will work out, you'll see. Give it time, my love, give it time.'

'I want to go back to England,' cried Amie, shaking her head and trying to free herself. 'I can't stop here now, I can't! I'm going to sell. I'm going to ring the lawyers right now and put it in their hands.'

Mrs Hobbs returned to her chair and looked at Amie sadly. 'You're making a big mistake, you won't solve anything by running away.'

Amie had never felt so distraught. 'I don't care, I'm catching the next plane back to London. I can't face Oliver after this. I'm sorry you've had this journey for nothing.'

'And I'm sorry I told you about him,' said Hobby. 'I feel it's all my fault.' She poured Amie a cup of tea and heaped sugar into it. 'Here, love, drink this. Give yourself time to think clearly, don't be too hasty.'

Reluctantly Amie sat and drank the tea, staring distractedly into space. She was paying the penalty for the accident, that was for certain—first her hand and now this. It made her wonder what else fate held in store. Was her whole life to be one perpetual living hell?

Eventually she calmed down sufficiently to think rationally, but she did not change her mind about selling. 'In that case,' said Hobby practically, 'sell to Oliver Maxwell. You have a ready-made buyer there, no trouble, no waiting.'

'No!' On that point Amie was adamant. 'I won't sell to him. It's what he's wanted all along, he'll think he's won.' Two spots of high colour appeared in her cheeks and her green eyes flashed with the light of battle. 'I shan't tell him it's on the market. He won't know anything about it until it's too late.'

Hobby shook her head yet again, but said nothing, apparently realising at this stage that Amie would listen to no one, and when her young friend left the room to make her arrangements she quietly got on with the washing up.

Amie returned to the kitchen some minutes later and looked across at Hobby's back as she worked at the sink. 'It's all fixed,' she said, and felt a bit put out when the woman did not turn. 'Mr Atkinson's going to put it into the hands of an estate agent. He said it shouldn't take long, and I've booked us both a flight for tomorrow.'

'I see.' Hobby sounded flat.

Amie said, 'I'm sorry, Hobby, I know you can't understand how I feel, but it's all for the best, I'm sure of that.'

The other woman's shoulders lifted in a disapproving shrug. 'It's your life you're ruining.'

Amie felt like crying and, turning, she dashed
from the room. She had never felt so alone in her
life.

Lunch was a silent affair, and soon after it was
over a taxi appeared at the door. Mrs Hobbs said,
'I'm going to see something of the island before I
go back. I haven't come all this way for nothing.
You can come with me, if you like.'

Amie didn't like, but it would be better than
spending the afternoon here on her own, she supposed. She had already done her packing, there
was nothing else left to do.

Hobby enjoyed their sightseeing tour, exclaim-
ing time and time again as they rounded bends
and experienced breathtaking views of mountains,
gorges, woodland, and above all the placid sea-
lagoons with their glorious mixture of indigo, royal
blue and turquoise.

'It's like paradise,' she sighed ecstatically. 'You
would leave all this because you're afraid of one
man?'

'I'm not afraid of him,' retorted Amie indignantly.

'No?' Hobby raised her pale brows, her round
eyes sceptical.

'Well,' Amie shrugged, 'not very much, but I
don't want to see him again.'

'You're prepared to forgo your love for him just
because of what you think *he'll* think? You can't
know that he'll blame you, I would say that there's
a ninety-nine per cent chance that he won't.'

And it's the one per cent I'm frightened of,

thought Amie. 'You forget he's already got it in for me because I went out with his chief engineer against his wishes.'

'And since you've already told me the reason why,' insisted Hobby, 'it's no excuse. All you two need is the chance to get together, have a good talk and sort everything out.'

'It still wouldn't do any good,' sighed Amie. 'He doesn't love me. The only reason he's shown any interest is because he's after Shangri-La.'

'Are you sure?'

'I'm positive.'

Mrs Hobbs sighed. 'Then you most probably are doing the right thing. I'm sorry it's happened like this, it could have been perfect.'

It was growing dark when they returned to the house. They both felt weary and decided a sandwich would suffice instead of dinner, and then early to bed ready for their long journey tomorrow.

Mrs Hobbs pushed Amie into the drawing room. 'Sit down—I'll see to supper, it won't take long.'

Amie subsided limply on to a chair, not bothering to switch on the lights. She felt now as she had after the accident, as though life was not worth living any more. Well, it wasn't, was it, not when the man she loved was the one person who had the best reason to hate her?

She closed her eyes and allowed herself to wallow in her misery. Thank goodness it would all soon be over, that she could take up her life again in London, such as it was, without the risk of bumping into Oliver Maxwell. There had to be some job she could do somewhere. She hadn't really bothered to find out before; now all she wanted

was work, something to keep her mind occupied,
something to—— Her thoughts were interrupted
when a voice sounded at the other end of the
room.

'I've been waiting for you.'

At first she had thought it was Marcel, and a cold
terror gripped her, but as he spoke she knew differently and she stared at the shadowy shape that
was coming slowly towards her, unable to move,
unable to speak, a different kind of fear taking
over.

It took a few long moments for her to realise
that Oliver couldn't possibly know yet about her
involvement in the accident, not until Hobby
appeared on the scene. Then he would draw his
conclusions and—— She shuddered. Somehow she
had to get rid of him before Mrs Hobbs came in
with their sandwiches.

'What do you want?' she asked in a hoarse whisper.

'Who've you been out with? Marcel?' he enquired abruptly. 'And whose was that voice I
heard just now?—it wasn't Peta?'

'It's another woman I've got,' she improvised
hastily. 'Peta left, and I couldn't cope on my own.'

The room was suddenly flooded with light. She
blinked and looked defiantly across at him. 'If I
go out with Marcel that's my affair,' she added.
'He's the only civilised person around here.'

Inside she was crying. What had happened to her
confession, why didn't she tell him the truth?
Hobby was right when she said all they needed
to do was talk, but how could she, when Oliver
was looking at her as though she was unclean?

She felt his hatred cut through her like a knife; it had not lessened with his being away. 'So that's the way it is,' he said tightly. 'I just hope you know what you're doing. Marcel won't marry you if you get pregnant.'

He even thought she had slept with him! It got worse. 'I'm not so foolish as to let that happen.' Her brilliant eyes dared him to argue.

'No?' Clearly he did not believe her. 'I know for a fact that you spent one night with him, yet you're trying to tell me he didn't take you to bed? I'm not an idiot, Amie, so don't class me as one.'

So it had been Oliver who phoned, and getting no answer he had arrived at the conclusion she had expected. What good would it do to deny it now? None at all, judging by the mood he was in. He had apparently been brooding over it all the while he was in London.

'You're not my keeper, for heaven's sake,' she snapped, 'so don't try acting like one. Now you've had your say perhaps you'll go. I've had a long day and I'm tired.'

Oliver too looked suddenly weary, and somehow disappointed, though she couldn't think why. 'I will,' he said, 'now I've had my suspicions confirmed. I'm disappointed in you, Amie, I thought you were above that sort of thing.'

'I am,' she wanted to cry out, 'I am, if you would only listen.' But what was the use? Nothing she could say now would make any difference. She had more or less admitted to having an affair with Marcel. If she tried to deny it now he would think she was lying to save her own face.

'Goodnight, Oliver,' she said quietly, and to herself, 'Goodbye,' because this was probably the last time she would see him, and it hurt that she should remember him like this with his face tightly disapproving, his blue eyes cold and distant.

She watched as he opened the door and left the room, and if he had looked back he would have seen the love shining on her face, but he didn't. He closed the door none too gently and a few seconds later she heard the front door open and close. He had gone. It was the end. She felt as though she wanted to kill herself.

A few minutes later Hobby came bustling in with a loaded tray. 'I thought I heard voices,' she said brightly, looking about the room as if to see someone hiding in a corner.

'You did,' agreed Amie flatly. 'Oliver Maxwell.'

'Oh,' said Hobby, and nearly dropped the tray. 'What happened? He didn't stay long.'

'That was because I didn't want him to. I wanted him out before he saw you, before he could destroy me altogether.'

Mrs Hobbs' lips drew into a prim line. 'Don't exaggerate,' she said sharply. 'I'm sure Mr Maxwell's a reasonable man, did you talk to him? Did you sort anything out at all?'

Amie shook her head slowly, wearily. 'He accused me of having an affair with Marcel. I think he came here to confirm what he already suspected.'

'And you denied it, of course?'

The wide green eyes Amie turned on her friend were lifeless. 'No, there was no point.'

Mrs Hobbs sat down heavily, her face creased with anxiety. 'You're a silly child, Amie. You're making matters worse.'

'Am I?' asked Amie dully. 'It's impossible, they're already as bad as they can get.'

Ever practical, Hobby poured the tea and passed a cup to Amie. 'Why is youth so stubborn?' she said half to herself. 'If you could see life through my eyes you would realise that there's no sense in wasting time arguing, saying hurtful things to one another. You'd sort out your problems—life's too short not to live every second to the full.'

Amie knew she was thinking of her husband who had died suddenly, unexpectedly, before they had done half the things they planned. But it was difficult to see things through another person's eyes, especially when she knew herself that there was no hope, that nothing she could say would alter Oliver's opinion. All she hoped now was that he would not turn up again before they left tomorrow.

Her prayers were for once answered, and they arrived in cold wet London in the early hours, Hobby strangely withdrawn, evidently of the opinion that Amie was doing the wrong thing, and Amie no less happier now that she had fled the lion's den.

She had thought that she would feel better away from him, but this didn't prove to be the case. The days dragged interminably, she hadn't even the enthusiasm to go job-hunting. Hobby looked after her as though she was her own, watching as Amie's pretty face changed into a hollow image of her former self, not mentioning Mauritius or Oliver Maxwell, realising that Amie must solve her problem for herself.

It did not help that Shangri-La was proving

more difficult to sell than she had expected. She rang the lawyers almost daily, only to hear that there was no news, that the property was too big for a private buyer, but not large enough for a hotel, at least not on the scale that most of the enterprises demanded. It could be expanded, she debated, but it appeared no one was willing to do this. 'If it had been on the coast,' was the argument, 'it would have been ideal, but where it was— well...' They left her to draw her own conclusions.

It was several weeks before she had a call to say that it had been sold, that the contracts were ready for signing the next day, and would she please be present.

She told Hobby the good news and it was as though a weight had been lifted from her shoulders. From now on she could forget all about Shangri-La and Mauritius and Oliver Maxwell. It was a painful interlude in her life that was over. At long last she could start afresh.

When Amie duly presented herself at Mr Atkinson's offices she was a shadow of the girl who had turned up there several months earlier, full of enthusiasm and zest for what she had thought would prove the turning point in her life. It had done that, but not in the way she had expected.

Hobby offered to accompany her, but Amie had refused. 'This is something I shall enjoy doing,' she replied brightly, 'one thing I shall never regret.' But the moment she was shown into the sombre chambers by an equally sombre secretary Amie wished she had the other woman's support.

The last person she had expected to see sitting there, coolly smoking a cheroot and with a light of triumph in his eyes, was Oliver Maxwell. 'You!' she accused faintly, leaning back against the door and closing her eyes.

'Are you all right, Miss Douglas? Here, please sit down.' The lawyer's anxious voice penetrated the mist which fogged her mind. She hoped it was all a bad dream, that when she opened her eyes it would be some other person who sat there, someone resembling Oliver. It couldn't be him, it couldn't. Yet why not? He was the obvious person, except that she hadn't been aware he knew she had put Shangri-La on the market.

She made herself look again, forcing her eyes open as though they had been stuck with glue. It was Oliver all right, and if the lawyer was concerned for her wellbeing he most certainly was not. He was actually smiling, enjoying the shock he had given her. 'We meet again. You look surprised. Weren't you expecting me?'

Amie slid into the chair that was offered, staring at him hostilely, life flowing back into her limbs and with it a cold furious anger. 'I most certainly was not,' and to Mr Atkinson, 'Why didn't you tell me it was Mr Maxwell? I could have saved you all this trouble. I won't sell to him, not in a thousand years!' Her eyes alighted on an official-looking document on his desk. 'Is that the contract?' and before his astonished eyes she snatched it up and tore it across the middle, depositing the two halves on Oliver's lap.

He looked up at her, a mocking smile curving his lips, although his eyes were dangerously cold. 'If you want to sell Shangri-La, Miss Douglas, you have no choice. There are no other potential buyers. You'll be left with the proverbial white elephant if you don't sell to me.'

'Then I'll keep it,' she cried frantically.

'Why, if you don't intend living in it? It will fall to rack and ruin, and what will you get for it then?'

The lawyer butted in anxiously, 'Mr Maxwell's offer is more than generous, Miss Douglas. If I were you I'd think carefully before you reject it completely.'

'I already have,' she said tightly.

'So you're prepared to see it fall to pieces simply to stop me getting my hands on it?' Oliver spoke crisply, impatiently.

'No,' she said, making up her mind there and then and not stopping to think of the consequences. 'I shall go back there.' She thought too much of the house to let it decay.

'And live on what?' asked Oliver coldly. 'A cripple like you will never be able to earn enough money to run it.'

He had hurt her in the way that mattered most. Amie felt something snap inside her and lashed out, forgetting the white-collared man sitting stiffly at the other side of the desk.

Instinctively she had used her right arm and Oliver caught her wrist, looking down at the limp white fingers. 'Useless,' he said softly, mercilessly, and threw the hand from him in disgust.

Mr Atkinson was looking scandalised, clearly never having such a scene take place in his chambers before. 'I think it would be best if you both left,' he said frigidly. 'Let me know, Miss Douglas, what you intend doing. I shall charge you, of course, for the considerable inconvenience you have caused me.'

'Very well.' She felt a little ashamed to have behaved like this in his presence. 'But I can tell you here and now that I've decided to keep Shangri-La. I'm sorry to have put you to all this trouble.'

Oliver too got to his feet, pulling a wad of notes from his wallet. He placed them on Mr Atkinson's desk. 'I think that should cover everything. Good day.'

Amie was about to protest that she wanted no help from him when he caught her elbow in a vice-like grip and led her from the room. Once outside he let her go. 'So it looks like we're to be neighbours again. I must tell Marcel the good news. He was asking after you, you know, most surprised when I said you'd left. Why did you leave without telling anyone?'

The abrupt question surprised her and she had no time to think up a convincing reply. She shrugged. 'Let's say I got fed up.'

'With what—Marcel?' His eyes narrowed. 'Did things begin to get out of hand, is that why you ran?'

She shook her head; it felt heavy on her shoulders. 'That's not the reason, but I wouldn't expect you to believe the real one, so I'm not going to try.'

They were outside now on the street. 'Where do you live?' he asked suddenly. 'I'll give you a lift.'

'I'll catch the bus,' she said quickly. 'I should hate to put you out.' But most of all she dreaded him meeting Mrs Hobbs again and all that that meeting would entail.

'It's no trouble,' he said firmly, leading her towards his parked car. It was a Mercedes, nothing like the sports car he drove in Mauritius. Amie supposed it was hired, and sighed as she settled against the luxurious leather upholstery. What money could do for you! And why had Oliver inherited it instead of her? This was a thought that rankled. Perhaps if she had met her Uncle Philippe she would have known why.

As they neared the house Amie felt more and more uneasy. Her stomach was a tight ball and her heart pounded at twice its normal rate. When they pulled up outside Oliver looked at her questioningly. 'Is this it?'

She nodded and got out. 'Thanks for the lift. Goodbye, Mr Maxwell, I expect we'll be seeing each other again one day.'

But he got out too and followed her into the house. 'It wouldn't be very polite to accept my lift home and then not invite me in for coffee,' he said, when she attempted to stop him.

She sighed and went upstairs to her rooms, keeping her fingers crossed that Hobby would not hear them and come up to see how she had got on. With a bit of luck Oliver might think that she was a new lodger here; he might not guess that this was where she had lived before going to Mauritius.

He sat down and watched as she reached cups and saucers, unscrewed the lid off the coffee by holding the jar cradled in her right arm, and filled the kettle by standing it in the sink. All these tricks she had learned and could usually manage with no trouble, but because Oliver was watching her, because she was sure that Oliver knew who she was, she became nervous and clumsy, breaking a cup, dropping the jar of coffee, letting the kettle over-fill, and in the end she turned to him with tears in her eyes. 'Go on, say it, damn you, say what you're thinking!'

'I'm not thinking anything,' he said coolly, 'except that you're unusually clumsy. I would have offered to help, but I thought you'd refuse.'

A discreet tap on the door before it opened prevented Amie from giving him his answer. 'Amie, I heard noises, I didn't know you'd returned. How did—oh, Mr Maxwell, I didn't see you sitting there.'

Hobby looked considerably shocked, almost as much as Amie had when confronted by him in Mr Atkinson's office.

'Mr Maxwell was the buyer,' said Amie quickly, before Hobby could speak again. 'I refused, of course. There was no way I would sell to him. I'm going back to Mauritius. I'm going to keep Shangri-La after all.'

'And turn it into a hotel?' asked Hobby eagerly.

Amie willed her to be quiet.

'What did I tell you?' continued the little woman unconcernedly. 'It's perfect. In no time at all we'll be running a thriving business.'

Oliver looked from one to the other, waited until Hobby had finished, and then said, 'May I be permitted to ask how you know so much about Shangri-La, Mrs Hobbs?'

'Oh, didn't Amie tell you? I came over to Mauritius. You weren't there, of course, you were still in London.'

'Hobby,' hissed Amie distractedly, 'shut up!'

The woman stopped immediately. 'You've not told him?'

'That's right,' but even as she spoke Amie knew that what she had feared most was about to happen.

'Hobby?' Oliver mused. 'I should have realised. This is where you lived before.' And then on a sudden accusing note, 'You were the one who was driving the car, the one who——' His face was white now, eyes blazing like two silver lights.

'That's right!' screamed Amie, unable to stand the tension any longer. 'I killed your sister, I admit it. But I couldn't help it, and I've suffered—with this——' she waved her crippled hand in front of him, 'and I shall go on suffering for the rest of my life!' Tears were streaming down her face, but she ignored them. 'Call me what you like, think what you like, nothing can hurt me any more. I've had as much as I can stand!' She sank down on to the floor, curling into a ball, sobs racking her body. 'I wish I'd died too, do you know that?—anything would be better than this hell I've lived through ever since!'

Oliver did not speak again; he left the room, and as if from a distance Amie heard his car move away down the street. Hobby left her where she was for a few moments, busily making the cup of tea which was her cure for all ills. Then she helped the broken girl to her feet, guiding her to the divan which served as her bed at night. 'Drink this,' she said, 'you'll feel better soon.'

When Amie felt she could trust herself to speak she said, 'He blames me, Hobby, I knew he would.'

'Now then, love,' soothed her landlady. 'He didn't say that at all.'

'But he thought it,' she choked. 'How can I go back there now, how can I ever face him knowing that he sees me as his sister's murderer?'

'I'll be with you,' said Hobby. 'You'll always have my shoulder to cry on, but somehow I don't think it will come to that. I know he's a hard man, but he also strikes me as being fair, and once he's had time to give the matter some thought he'll realise that you're in no way to blame. As a matter of fact we don't even know he does blame you—he hasn't said in so many words.'

'Then why did he rush off?' cried Amie. 'Why didn't he reassure me that he held me in no way responsible? He knew what I was thinking. What does he want, for me to kill myself, is that what he'd like best?'

Mrs Hobbs took the cup from Amie's shaking hand, then she pulled the girl into her arms, holding her close, smoothing her hair and murmuring quietly as one would to a baby. 'There, there, my love, you're distraught, you don't know what you're saying. Let me help you undress. You must sleep. I've some tablets downstairs that the doctor gave me when Fred died—take one of those, you'll feel much better when you wake up.'

Amie nodded. 'Thank you, Hobby. I know I'm a nuisance, but I can't help it, really I can't.' The thought of sleep was tempting, even in the middle of the day. At least for a few hours she would get relief. She tried not to think that once she awoke the pain would still be there. Hobby would look after her, as she had after the accident. Hobby would always be there.

It was with her dear Hobby's face looking down

on her that Amie fell into a deep dreamless sleep, from which she did not awake until early the next morning.

The room was empty. She climbed out of bed and looked at herself in the mirror over the kitchen sink. She did not look too bad, not as dreadful as she had expected, and when she turned Hobby was there.

'I've been listening for you,' she smiled. 'I don't need to ask how you feel, you're looking much better, more like my normal Amie. Ready to fight, are you? You'd better be, because while you were asleep yesterday afternoon I was busy. I've booked our flights back to Mauritius, and this time there's no returning. We're going to make a go of it out there, if it's the last thing we do!'

CHAPTER NINE

DESPITE misgivings Amie could not deny the fact that she was happy to be back in Mauritius. Shangri-La had become home to her, and as soon as they arrived she wandered from room to room savouring the feeling of ownership, the fact that all this belonged to her, and in no way was she going to let anyone take it away, especially Oliver Maxwell.

When she realised how near she had come to selling it to him she felt a cold shiver run down her spine, at the same time mentally squaring her shoulders ready to do battle.

It was becoming a personal feud, but with Mrs Hobbs on her side Amie felt confident that they would win. It would not ruin Shangri-La, turning it into a hotel, in fact it would probably be the best thing that had happened to the place. It was a shame for so many rooms to lie empty, and she could only assume that her uncle must have done a lot of entertaining in his time, for otherwise, having no family, why would he have bought such a large house?

They had been there for less than an hour when the doorbell rang. Amie felt suddenly apprehensive and glanced quickly at Hobby. 'Who do you think that is?' she asked, even though she knew in her own mind. He must have been waiting for their arrival, watching the house, ready to make sure they did not go ahead with their plans to turn it into a hotel.

She let Hobby answer, resolutely remaining in the kitchen, hoping that she would send him away. They had been on the point of going to bed, ready for a few hours' sleep after their exhausting journey.

But she might have known Oliver would not take no for an answer. He came into the kitchen first, standing over her as though she was an errant child. Hobby followed and resumed her seat at the table.

'So you've come,' he said distantly. 'I didn't think you would, not after our—er—enlightening meeting.'

Amie stared at him coldly, glad he could not see

her inner turmoil. Even when he was angry with her it did not alter what she felt. Her love was such that no matter what he said, or what he thought of her, it would never die.

An electric tingle ran through her as she looked at him and she wanted nothing more than to beg his forgiveness and feel his arms about her, let his strength flow into her. But she knew that this could never be, and she willed herself to remain cool and indifferent. 'I see no reason, Mr Maxwell, why I shouldn't. It's my home, in case you'd forgotten.'

'I'm hardly likely to do that,' he returned icily, 'and since your conscience apparently doesn't bother you, perhaps you'll heed my warning that I propose objecting to whatever plans you might submit to turn this place into a hotel.'

'On what grounds?' she asked levelly.

He held her gaze for a few long seconds. 'That's my affair, Miss Douglas.'

And that was as much as he would tell her. He had no grounds, there was nothing he could do; he was just trying to frighten her. She looked across at Hobby for support.

The older woman smiled. 'Will you stay for a cup of tea, Mr Maxwell?'

Amie could have killed her.

He said, 'Oliver, please—and yes, I'd love to,' and sat down, his bulk dwarfing the table. 'I understand your husband was out here many years ago, Hobby—I may call you that? A pity you were never able to come out together.'

'What is to be will be,' she said philosophically. 'I'm of the firm opinion, Oliver, that our life is preordained and that no matter what we do or try to do it makes no difference. If we're meant to do a certain thing then we do, if we're not—well, we don't. Clearly I was not destined to come out here with Fred, but the good Lord wanted me to see it, and here I am.'

Amie thought he might attempt to make fun of Hobby, but he didn't. He nodded slowly, as though understanding perfectly. 'I agree with you, to a certain extent, but I also think that we ourselves have a say in what happens, that we can channel our lives along a certain path.'

'No, that's not true,' replied Hobby, warming to her subject. 'After my Fred died I was quite sure I would spend the rest of my life in London. I was quite content to stay there and take in lodgers and earn a few pounds that way. I never dreamt I would end up here.'

'Let's hope you're right,' he said, and Amie detected a softening in his manner, although when he looked at her his eyes were still disapproving. She had not expected anything else but could not help feeling disappointed.

He and Hobby monopolised the conversation. Amie sat and listened and felt more and more dejected. In the end she yawned deliberately and said, 'If you two don't mind I'm going to bed.'

Oliver immediately scraped back his chair and unfolded his long body. 'I'm sorry if I've kept you two up, I'd forgotten you'd had a tiring journey.' But it was Hobby to whom he addressed himself, Amie he ignored. She wanted to scream and say, 'Hey, I'm here! Don't forget, this is my home, I'm your hostess.'

But of course he had every reason to ignore her;

she was forgetting that. He blamed her for his sister's accident and she guessed that he would take great delight in future in making her life as uncomfortable as possible.

When he had gone Hobby said, 'There, he's not such a bad man after all, when you get talking to him.'

'I'm glad you like him,' said Amie, tight-lipped, 'you're welcome. I've decided I hate him.'

'Don't talk nonsense,' snapped Hobby impatiently. 'It's natural he'll resent you, for a while, but he'll get over it. In no time at all you'll be the best of friends.'

'We were never that,' retorted Amie, 'even before he found out about Ginny. He's always been against me for some reason. Probably because I've got Shangri-La and he wants it.'

'Then marry the man,' laughed her companion, 'that way you'll both get what you want.'

There was nothing Amie would like better, but it was farcical even to think about it. Oliver would never ask her to marry him; he had only ever shown interest because he had thought to force her into selling. She wondered whether he would still pursue this line or whether he had at last taken the hint, knowing that she was resolute.

Once she had had a night's sleep Amie felt better, more able to face whatever obstacles Oliver might put her way. She had not realised that they would have to get permission to use Shangri-La as a hotel. In her ignorance she had thought that all they had to do was advertise, and that was that. Their first course, then, was to go into Port Louis and fill in the necessary forms, and while they were waiting for approval they could begin to get the house ready. It would be fun, with Hobby to help.

They decided to catch a bus into Port Louis, rather than order a taxi. Amie had noticed that one ran past the gates every morning and it was while they were waiting for this that Oliver drove by in his sports car.

He stopped immediately he saw them. 'Can I give you a lift?' He directed his question at Hobby, avoiding looking at Amie, and she felt despair creeping through her yet again.

Would it help, she wondered, if she made some attempt at an apology? Perhaps he was waiting for her to bring the subject up. But she shrank from the thought; it could only cause unpleasantness. Far better if they ignored each other, at least then there was no chance of them arguing.

'We're going into Port Louis,' said Mrs Hobbs happily. 'Can you fit us both in?'

'If one of you doesn't mind curling up in the back.'

Amie couldn't let Hobby cramp herself, so she climbed awkwardly into the limited space behind the two seats, assuring Oliver that she was perfectly all right, though she wasn't, and he knew it, and he smiled with grim delight.

Hobby was as voluble as always and she and Oliver carried on an animated conversation while Amie herself grew increasingly irritated and uncomfortable and hoped the journey wouldn't last much longer. It hadn't seemed to take this long when Oliver brought her before, but then she had been happy, had hardly noticed the passing of time, content in his company.

Now everything had changed, there was no way that she would ever feel at ease with him again. She suddenly realised that Oliver was asking Mrs Hobbs why they were going into Port Louis. 'Don't tell him!' she wanted to cry, but it was too late, already the older woman had in all innocence confessed that they were going to see about getting approval to turn Shangri-La into a hotel.

'Perhaps you can tell us where to go,' she suggested brightly.

Amie cringed and waited for his reply.

'I'll do more than that, I'll take you right there,' he said, and she nearly died of shock. Oliver helping them! She couldn't believe it. There had to be some ulterior motive behind his apparent courteousness.

They soon found out. 'You can make an application by all means,' said the polite clerk behind the counter. 'But I can tell you now that it will be a waste of time.'

'Why?' asked Amie indignantly. 'It's perfect for a hotel, and it belongs to me, so why shouldn't I do what I want with it?'

The clerk said patiently, 'We'd already had some intimation that you might be approaching us regarding this matter, and we've had several objections lodged with us—very valid ones, I may say.'

'From whom?' questioned Amie hotly, although she knew without a shadow of doubt who it would be. No wonder Oliver had been so eager to bring them here; he had known what the outcome of their visit would be. He could have saved them the trouble had he so wanted, but no, he was taking a perverse delight in making her suffer. How she hated him!

'I am not at liberty to disclose this,' replied the young man. 'I am sorry, Miss Douglas, but that's the position. Are you still going to try?'

She jutted her chin determinedly. 'Yes,' she replied, to his obvious surprise. 'I'm as keen to open my house as a hotel as whoever it is is determined to oppose me. Let's say it will be a case of the best man winning.'

By the look on his face it would not be her, observed Amie, but she did not care. Even if she lost it would not be so bad as sitting back and admitting defeat. For all she knew Oliver might back down when he saw how resolute she was.

They spent a pleasant two hours after that looking round the shops and then, miraculously, as they waited at the bus stop, Oliver again put in an appearance. Amie decided he had been hanging around purposely, ready to gloat over their defeat.

'Say nothing,' she hissed to Hobby, nudging her with her elbow. 'Leave it to me if he asks any questions.'

She smiled brightly at him as she folded herself carefully into the back of his car. 'This is very kind of you, Mr Maxwell,' she said. 'We really weren't looking forward to the long bus ride. It's so hot and we've not yet got acclimatised.'

He looked at her suspiciously, and she wondered if he knew that it was all an act, or whether he was beginning to entertain doubts that their trip had not been so unsuccessful as he had hoped.

Certainly if he had expected them both to look crestfallen he had been mistaken. Hobby was as cheerful as Amie and began talking about the amazing conglomeration of shops and nationalities, of the fascinating statues that were dotted about the town and in particular the market place, which Amie had not seen on her first visit.

'It's enchanting,' she continued chirpily, 'like a casbah with its high walls and entrance gate. We've bought all sorts of things.' She indicated her bulging shopping basket which she had settled between her knees. 'Freshly baked loaves, fruit, a few souvenirs—oh, and we had one of those chilli cakes, what did he call them, Amie?' she asked carelessly over her shoulder.

Carry on, thought Amie, you're doing fine. At this rate he won't have time to get a word in before we arrive back home. '*Gateaux piments*,' she supplied readily, and listened with increasing amusement as Hobby rattled on at a fine pace.

Nor did he, but one thing spoiled it. For ever hospitable, Hobby said, when they got back, 'Won't you come in, Oliver? You've been so kind perhaps you'd like to join us for dinner.'

'Indeed I would,' he said, glancing at Amie through the mirror as he spoke and seeing the sudden flash of resentment which crossed her face. 'That is, if Miss Douglas doesn't mind?'

'Do I have any choice?' She was being petty, but she couldn't help it. Why had Hobby to spoil everything like this, just when she thought they had got away without being cross-questioned?

'It's your house,' he said deferentially.

'I'm glad you've remembered,' she replied coolly, 'but since Hobby's already issued the invitation I won't be so cruel as to say no.'

'But you wouldn't have asked me if it had been left to you?'

She stared haughtily at the silver-blue eyes watching her closely. 'I think you know the answer to that.'

The eyes narrowed and then slanted across at the older woman. Amie held her breath, thinking that perhaps after all he was going to turn down her offer, but no. 'What rare delicacy do you have in mind?' he questioned lightly. 'Fish, perhaps?'

'How did you guess?' asked Mrs Hobbs, surprised.

He laughed and looked down at her bag. 'They do have a rather pungent smell, don't you think?'

While Hobby cooked their dinner Amie was compelled to keep Oliver company. She had tried to get out of it, but the other woman insisted, and now the two of them sat out on the terrace, sipping their pre-dinner drinks.

She felt him watching her, studying her carefully with those intense silvery eyes, and a quiver of fear ran through her. She would much rather have had Oliver as a friend than an enemy. She felt ill at ease, waiting for him to fire some barbed comments.

If she hadn't loved him it wouldn't hurt quite so much, she would be able to give as good as she got, but feeling as she did she was aware of the antagonism directed towards her, of the loathing and blame, and it hurt like nothing else ever had.

'How did your business go?' he asked at length. 'Successfully, I hope?'

'Don't say things you don't mean,' she snapped. 'You know damn well that you've already made your feelings known, but don't think it's stopping me, because it's not. I've lodged my application, and if it's a case of doing battle with you, Mr Maxwell, then I shall. In fact I shall find it quite amusing to see your face when we eventually open as a hotel.'

'I've no doubt you will,' he said, and sighed, and she couldn't understand why.

She had expected some form of retaliation, had braced herself for the ensuing argument. It was disappointing to discover he had appeared to accept that she might win. 'Is that all you've got to say?' she queried dubiously.

'What did you expect—a verbal battle? Not at the moment, I prefer to wait and see what happens. One of us is in for a big surprise.'

Amie wondered whether Oliver knew something that she didn't. He certainly did not look too perturbed. She glared furiously, entirely unprepared when he abruptly changed the subject.

'Marcel's been asking after you again.'

She jerked her head sharply. 'You told him I'm back?'

He nodded. 'I thought you'd want him to know.'

'Well, I didn't,' she snapped.

'What's happened to the friendship, gone sour already?' he goaded.

'There never was any particular friendship.' Now was her chance to explain, but before she could even begin he returned scathingly:

'You expect me to believe that? What do you take me for, Amie, a complete idiot? I saw you together, don't forget, and Marcel himself has wasted no time in telling me what good *friends* you've become.'

'And you believe his word rather than mine?' she asked bitterly.

'Is there any reason why I shouldn't?' He set down his empty glass and put his hands behind his head, leaning back and looking at her enigmatically so that she had no way of knowing whether he really did believe Marcel. Though why he should believe a man like that when he knew the type of character he was was beyond her.

'There's every reason in the world,' she returned primly, 'but it's all too clear that you're not prepared to listen. You've drawn your own conclusions and that's it so far as you're concerned. You believe what you've seen with your own eyes and have never stopped to think that things might not be what they seem.'

Oliver snorted derisively. 'When a woman goes out with a man, especially someone like Marcel, it's usually only for one reason. He's damned attractive, I admit, he can have the pick of any girl he likes, if they don't object to providing the entertainment he demands.'

'You still think I went to bed with him?' Amie felt colour flood her cheeks, though not for the reason he assumed. He took it as a sign of guilt and his lips tightened dramatically.

'Every picture tells a story,' he quoted drily. 'I must admit I'm disappointed. I didn't think you were that sort of girl.'

'Appearances can be misleading,' she said angrily. 'I'm sorry you've decided I'm not the innocent English rose after all.' She finished her drink and crashed down the glass. 'Why are you here?' she demanded heavily. 'Do you get a sordid kind of

pleasure out of humiliating me? Do you want to be
around when I fall?' She shook her head desperately. 'I shan't, don't worry. I might not have the
full use of all my limbs, but there's nothing wrong
with my brain and I'm staying on at Shangri-La,
and finding some way of financing it even if it kills
me!'

Oliver smiled calmly, his blue eyes placid,
apparently not in the least perturbed by her out-
burst. 'So that I won't have it? Yet you were prepared to sell to someone else. May I be permitted to
ask exactly what it is you have against me?'

What a laugh! As if she had anything against
him. She was dying slowly inside because he didn't
love her, that was what was the matter. Her own
love was insidiously eating away at her, making
her bitter, making her utter angry words that she
did not mean.

He took her silence as refusal. 'Very well, if
you're not prepared to tell me. I wonder what you'd
say if Marcel had put in an offer. Would you refuse
him as well, or would that be different? Actually
I'm amazed he hasn't moved in with you,' he
added. 'When I came back from London that first
time I fully expected to see him here. What sort
of a lover is he, Amie? Did he come up to your
expectations? Are Frenchmen as sexy as they're
reputed to be?'

'Shut up!' cried Amie jerkily, feeling tears all
too near the surface. 'You know nothing about it!'

'Then tell me,' he suggested insolently, abruptly
sitting up, leaning forward slightly and resting his
elbows on his knees, his hands clasped loosely between. 'I'm very interested.'

She glared, wondering how on earth she could love a man who persisted in treating her so abominably. Even now, while he was staring at her with an infuriatingly mocking expression, there emanated from him an aura of sensuality and she would need no second bidding to fling herself into his arms, offer herself to him regardless of consequences. Instead she took the only other way out. Rising swiftly to her feet, she swung her good hand towards his face.

He must have seen it coming, yet he made no attempt to avoid the blow. It was as though he never felt it, yet Amie's palm was stinging, and she experienced a great personal satisfaction. It would have been better if he had flinched, or cried out, or even called her names, but even so she had had the gratification of giving vent to her emotions.

They glowered at one another for a few long-drawn-out seconds. She had the feeling that she was not going to get away with this, but rather than face any delayed reprisal she turned on her heel. Her action goaded Oliver into movement and for a man so big he sprang up remarkably quickly and caught her arm, twisting her round to face him.

She was fascinated by his glittering silver eyes and drew in her breath sharply, half afraid, half expectant. 'Compare me,' he grated, before his mouth closed on hers in a brutally punishing kiss.

Immediate reaction spiralled through her and without thinking she pressed her body against him. For a brief space his mouth lifted, harsh words grated against her lips. 'Tell me how I compare with your Gallic friend, you little minx—I must know, do you hear, I must know!'

It was like a cry from his heart and Amie stifled a shudder. He sounded as though he hated her, desperately, furiously, yet if he did, why was he kissing her? Was degradation his intention? Was he expecting a response so that he could fling her from him in disgust, or was he trying to wreak revenge on Marcel, giving himself ammunition to fire at the other man?

Tears slid down her face, mingling with the bruising kisses; she tasted salt against her lips, yet all the time she was conscious of a longing bigger than herself. Even if it meant increasing his loathing she knew that she could not withdraw. She belonged here, body and soul, and he could do what he liked; she was as putty in his hands, weak, helpless, and completely his.

CHAPTER TEN

OLIVER'S kiss lasted so long that Amie began to feel faint; prickly heat covered her body, blood pounded in her head, and her arms dropped limply to her sides. Immediately he released her, staring down coldly as she fell back into the lounger he had previously occupied.

'Fickle!' he exploded. 'I'm disappointed but not surprised. It's perhaps fortunate that your uncle never discovered the real you.'

'Why bring him into it?' she questioned tiredly.
Her pulses still raced and her body cried out for
him. She ought to be hating him, but she didn't.
He was everything in a man that she wanted, tough,
determined, but with an undeniable charisma and
a sexual attraction that was like a call of the wild.
There was animal in him, barbaric, exciting, and
she wanted him for her mate. She wanted to make
love with a passionate abandonment, inhibitions
discarded, a fervent, exhilarating, sacred joining of
their two bodies as one.

'Because he's the reason I still show an interest
in you,' he said dispassionately. 'You remember that
it was his dearest wish that we marry? Ludicrous,
isn't it, under the circumstances. I want no tramp
as my wife. Uninterest I could have put up with
just about, there would perhaps have been a chance
of something growing out of it, but someone like
you, someone prepared to throw themselves at any
man who holds out his arms, that sticks in my
throat, *it makes me sick!*'

With that he walked away and a few minutes
later she heard his car as it roared down the drive.
Tears cascaded freely and she made no attempt to
dry them. Mrs Hobbs came bustling out. 'Was that
Oliver's car?' she asked before she had even reached
Amie. 'I thought he was——' The instant she saw
Amie she stopped. 'My dear girl, whatever's the
matter? You two been arguing again?'

Amie nodded dismally, and turned her head
away.

Hobby sighed. 'I don't know what's got into you,
Amie. I deliberately left you alone so that you

could sort out your problems. What have you been
saying to him?'

'What have *I* been saying?' Amie screamed indignantly. 'It's him! He's practically accused me
of being of easy virtue, that's what, and if you think
I was going to take that without a fight—well——'
She breathed deeply and furiously, clenching her
one good hand and pummelling it against the side
of her seat.

'You must have been mistaken,' insisted the
older woman, her button-bright eyes puzzled.
'You're no more immoral than—than I am.' She
smiled weakly at her own joke.

'Well, he thinks I am,' fumed Amie, pushing
herself up and marching into the house, leaving
her older friend to follow. 'Just because he saw
me out with Marcel! He has a filthy mind, if you
ask me!' The table was laid in the dining room and
she sat down heavily, scowling at her companion,
her beautiful green eyes clouded and angry.

'Why didn't you tell him that Marcel blackmailed you?' asked Hobby reasonably, joining Amie
at the table.

Amie's fine brows shot up. 'Would he have believed me? Like he would a child who says he hasn't
been eating strawberries but has tell-tale red all
round his mouth. He's got it in for me for some
reason.' She snorted derisively. 'You know what he
said? That it was my uncle's dream that we two
marry. Isn't that the funniest thing you've ever
heard? He couldn't have desired it very much, not
the way he's treated me. It amazes me really, it
would have been the easiest way for him to get his
hands on this house, and I, poor sucker, would have

fallen for any line he cared to shoot!'

Mrs Hobbs ate a mouthful of the grapefruit she had carefully prepared. 'Perhaps he doesn't believe in marriage without love.'

'Perhaps pigs will fly,' scoffed Amie, pushing her plate away savagely and leaping from the table. 'I'm going to my room—sorry about the food, but I'm not hungry.'

Even then it seemed that her troubles had not ended. No sooner had she reached her bedroom than she heard the phone ring. Hobby answered and then called up to Amie. 'It's for you, love. A man, says it's important.'

Oliver? Marcel? She wanted to speak to neither. 'Tell him I'm asleep,' she snapped.

'I've already told him you'd only just gone upstairs. I think you ought to answer, Amie. It's not Oliver. He sounds very charming, whoever he is.'

It had to be Marcel. Wearily Amie made her way back downstairs. 'Hello?' She injected no enthusiasm into her voice, leaning back against the wall and holding the phone as though it was a dead weight.

'Amie, it is Marcel. Welcome back.'

'I thought it might be you,' she said dispiritedly. 'What do you want?'

'Is that any way to greet an old friend?' he queried with pretended offence.

She looked at the receiver, almost as though it was him she was staring at. 'You're no friend of mine, I thought I'd made that clear.'

'You were offended because I tried to take advantage. I won't again, I assure you. Please come out with me, Amie, I've missed you.'

'Then you'll have to go on missing me, and if that's all you've rung for, I'm going. I'm tired. I was just about to have an early night.'

'At seven o'clock?' His surprise was genuine. 'Why, are you ill?'

I'm sick, she thought, sick of you, sick of Oliver, sick of everything. 'You could say that. I've had a tiring day in Port Louis. I'm not yet used to the heat.'

'You went with Oliver?' It was more an accusation than a question. Amie wondered how he had guessed.

'He gave us a lift, yes. We didn't arrange it, if that's what you're getting at.'

A fractional hesitation before he said, 'Did he say anything—about me?'

Amie became suddenly alert. Clearly Marcel had a guilty conscience. 'Why should he? He said you knew I was back, that was all. Why, what have you been saying?'

'Nothing.' The protestation was too quick to ring true.

'In any case it doesn't matter,' she said weakly, not realising how desperate she sounded. 'It's doubtful I shall see him again.'

'You have quarrelled?' Strangely he sounded concerned.

She sighed. 'Yes. He walked out on me, and in case you're interested it was all because of you.'

A long pause and then he asked, 'Where's Oliver now?'

'Why?' she asked sharply.

'I want to see him. Is he at home?'

'I've no idea,' she admitted. 'He drove away from here a quarter of an hour ago as though he was practising for the Monte Carlo rally. He could be anywhere.'

When the line went dead she was surprised, but not sufficiently concerned to let it bother her. She did wonder whether Marcel had some idea of trying to clear himself, but that was absurd. Even if he did succeed in convincing Oliver that he was not entirely the black character he was purported to be, it would make no difference so far as she was concerned. Their relationship had reached an irrevocable end. All she had to look forward to was the turning of Shangri-La into a hotel, and somehow even that felt flat; she had no fight in her any more. In fact she was almost tempted to sell to Oliver after all.

Hobby had hovered while she spoke to Marcel, there was no need to elucidate. 'I'm off to bed now,' Amie smiled weakly. 'If anyone else rings tell them I'm out, or asleep, or even dead.'

Mrs Hobbs was scandalised. 'Now, now, love, there's no need for talk like that! It's not the end of the world. I'll bring you up a cup of tea and a sleeping tablet. Mind you, I don't want you getting addicted to them, but—well, I daresay one won't hurt now and again.'

In the middle of the night Amie was woken by Mrs Hobbs roughly shaking her arm. 'What's the matter?' she asked thickly, still drugged by the effects of the tablet.

'There's a wind got up,' replied the other woman. She had pulled on an ancient cotton dressing gown over her nightdress and in Amie's befuddled state she looked like a ghost. 'I'm worried about it.'

Even as she spoke the noise of the wind was making itself heard. Amie dragged herself out of bed and made her way to the window. The trees were blowing beneath the force of the gusts, dust was eddying like great swirls of fog, and somewhere an open window could be heard banging.

'We must close the shutters,' she said, suddenly wide awake and in command of the situation. Without even bothering to pull on her own dressing gown she ran from room to room, and when they had finished upstairs they raced outside.

Here the wind tore at their clothes, whipping them round their legs and over their heads alternately. It took all their strength to fasten the shutters and slide the heavy bars into place, and before they had finished it began to rain.

The first thing they did when they got back inside was to change out of their wet clothes. 'I've never known winds like this,' said Hobby shakily, clearly upset by what was happening. 'Do they happen often?'

Amie shook her head. 'I don't think so, it's the first I've known, but I do seem to remember Oliver saying something about Mauritius being in the middle of the south Indian Ocean cyclone belt.'

It was the worst thing she could have said. Hobby sat down heavily on a chair. 'A cyclone? We could be killed!'

'I doubt it,' said Amie practically. 'More often than not the island only feels the fringe. I think the last bad one they had was about ten years ago. I'll put the radio on, apparently they issue warnings when cyclones are imminent.'

'I'd rather not hear,' whispered Hobby, her face pale, her eyes wide and scared, her straight hair sticking in wet spikes about her head.

The wind's velocity was increasing minute by minute and there was a crashing and tearing outside as though a tree had been uprooted and thrown against the walls of the house. It was accompanied by a banging on the door, and a barely discernible voice requesting to be let in.

'Oliver!' exclaimed Amie in relief.

She had scarcely drawn the bolt when the door was whipped back by the tremendous gale force winds, wrenched off its hinges and flung across the hall, smashing into pieces against the wall and bringing down with it several of the pictures Amie so admired.

'Damn!' swore Oliver. 'I should have warned you to hold on tight, but thank goodness you're all right, and that you had the presence of mind to fasten the shutters.' His shirt and trousers clung like a second skin to his powerful body, his hair, darkened by the rain, plastered close to his head. 'Where's Hobby? You can't stay here now, that's for certain, you must come back with me.'

'To your cabin?' asked Amie incredulously. 'Surely that won't be as safe as this. Can't we mend the door, wedge something against the opening, perhaps?' She had to shout to make herself heard above the shrieking of the wind.

'Don't be stupid,' he yelled back, 'where's your sense, woman? Besides, your roof could be ripped off at any second, you know it was already in need of repair, and with this wind coming in——'

As he spoke there was a tearing sound more awful

than anything Amie had ever heard and the wind rushed through the house like a vortex. Upstairs Hobby screamed and came stumbling down. 'The roof's gone, the roof's gone!' she cried hysterically. 'What are we going to do? This is the end and I'm not ready. I don't want to die, not like this!'

This was not typical of the sane Hobby they knew, and Oliver gave her one furious look before slapping her across the face. 'Sorry, Hobby, I have no choice. Calm down, nothing's going to happen to you. You're coming back with me.'

They had to fight their way out of the house, winds such as Amie had never experienced before pressing them back. It was like struggling against an immovable object. 'We'll never make it,' cried Hobby. 'Can't we stay?'

'And have the house fall about your ears?' asked Oliver harshly. 'There's worse to come. If we can make it to my bungalow we'll be safe. It's good and solid, nowhere near so fragile as this.'

'*If* we make it,' shrieked Hobby, her eyes bright with tears that mingled with the rain on her face. 'Is there any doubt?'

'There is if you stand here arguing,' yelled Oliver tersely. 'Grab hold of my arms, let's get going!'

Branches flew through the air and several times they narrowly missed being hit. Occasionally there was a lull; tense silent moments between gusts. They would take advantage of them to hurry forward, but in some way Amie found them even more frightening, knowing that the next blast could be worse.

They were risking their lives, taking a chance of being blown into the air themselves, so strong was the force of the wind, and she was grateful to Oliver for his concern. He could have remained in his own safe little bungalow without bothering to check up on them.

In a way it was his fault. If she hadn't opened the door to him they themselves might have been all right. It was the strength of the wind through the open doorway that had ripped off the roof, filling the house like a vacuum. But she knew that it was unfair thinking like this. The roof had been unsafe anyway. It would only have been a matter of time before it lifted. Oliver's appearance had precipitated matters, that was all.

Amie did not know how long it took them to reach Oliver's home. It seemed like hours, it was in fact probably about thirty minutes. But half an hour in that gale was like a lifetime.

His hurricane shutters were already in position and he barred and bolted the door quickly behind them. The relative calm was like an oasis in the desert and all three fell limply into the first available chairs.

Once they had recovered Oliver suggested they get out of their wet clothes and into something dry. 'But we've brought nothing with us,' insisted Mrs Hobbs. 'How can we?'

'You'll have to wear something of mine,' he returned drily, practically. 'I'm sorry there wasn't time to pack a case.'

'I'm sorry,' she said humbly. 'I'm being ungrateful. You've probably saved our lives, Oliver. Thank you.'

Amie and Hobby shared the bedroom while Oliver changed in the kitchen-cum-living room, and there was much amusement when they surveyed each other in trousers and shirts many times too large for them.

'You look like a clown,' laughed Amie, looking at her older friend in the rolled-up trousers and baggy shirt.

'You're not much better yourself,' defended Hobby, surveying the tightly belted jeans and white shirt, which Amie had tied in a knot at her waist, and then, 'No, that's not true, with your figure you look good in anything. I guess you'd even make a hessian sack look like a Dior dress.'

Amie smiled ruefully. 'What bothers me is that we've more than likely lost all our clothes. They've probably blown all over the island by now. I wonder what we're going to do?'

'There'll be many more in the same boat,' said Hobby in her best down-to-earth voice. 'At least we're safe, that's what matters.'

They joined Oliver and Mrs Hobbs busied herself making tea and cutting sandwiches. Amie sat opposite Oliver at the table and asked, 'What do you think will happen to Shangri-La? Will it be possible to repair it?'

'If there's anything left,' he returned drily. 'But I shouldn't worry, your insurance will cover it.'

Amie's heart contracted and she clapped a hand to her mouth.

He took one look at her and said harshly, 'Don't say you never renewed it? I did remind you that it was due.'

'I know.' She was almost in tears again now. 'But I kept putting it off. I couldn't really afford it, I never dreamt anything like this might happen.'

'No one ever does, until it's too late. You're an idiot, Amie. For the sake of a few hundred rupees you've lost your house. Everything you inherited has gone with no chance of it ever being recovered. How could you be so damned naïve?'

What could she say? Nothing, except look at him with her wide green eyes and trust he would relent.

He glared angrily and the noise of the merciless wind added emphasis to his fury.

Fortunately Mrs Hobbs interrupted their silent antagonism by handing round plates of sandwiches and steaming cups of tea. 'What a way to spend a night,' she said conversationally. 'I've done some things in my time, but never anything like this.'

His attention diverted, Oliver said, 'This is only the fringe of the cyclone. If the eye had passed right over the island then you really would have cause to be frightened. Even so the effects can be catastrophic. You're unlucky that it's happened while you're here. On an average we only have four days of winds such as this in any one year, and I believe there's only been twelve days of really bad weather in the last ninety years. So you see, the chances of your experiencing weather such as this were really very slim.'

'So why has Shangri-La suffered?' asked Amie petulantly. She was still very much hurt and angry with herself for not attending to the insurance.

'Because,' said Oliver patiently, 'it's been neglected. Your uncle's been ill over the past twelve months or so and hasn't bothered to carry out the repairs that would normally have been done as a matter of routine. A good solid well looked after house won't suffer, not in these sort of winds.'

For two days they remained in Oliver's bungalow while outside the wind howled and shrieked and caused havoc and destruction. On the third day, when the wind had abated slightly although by no means died away completely, Oliver said, 'I'll take a walk over to Shangri-La, see if there's anything left worth salvaging.'

'Can I come?' asked Amie immediately. She was fed up with being stuck in this tiny building.

'No!' He was adamant. 'It's not safe yet, you stay here with Hobby.'

Reluctantly Amie obeyed, but when several hours passed and he still had not returned she began to feel concerned for his safety. 'I'm going to see where he is,' she said decisively.

Mrs Hobbs looked worried. 'He said we were to stay here. He won't like it, you wandering around on your own.'

'But he might be hurt,' insisted Amie. 'I've got this feeling. I'm sure something has happened to him. I must go, Hobby, I must.'

'Then I'll come too.'

'No, you stay here in case we miss each other. You can tell him where I've gone.'

Without waiting for any more arguments Amie let herself out of the house, shouting to Hobby to bolt the door behind her.

The wind was nowhere near as strong as it had been, but it was sufficiently driving to make her pull her clothes tightly about her. The rain had ceased, but the scene of destruction that met her eyes was quite horrifying.

She had to pick her way across fallen trees and branches which clawed and tore at her trousers and shirt, and she was scratched and bleeding by the time she arrived at Shangri-La.

Shangri-La! All that was left was a heap of rubble. She was appalled. For as far as she could see in all directions were bits and pieces of what had once been the house. Her inheritance—totally destroyed! It was heartbreaking, and tears raced down her cheeks as she stood and observed, rooted to the spot.

There was no sign of Oliver and she was too disturbed to go any closer. She decided he must have gone on to the factory when he realised there was nothing he could do here. On the point of returning she heard a faint cry, borne to her on the waves of the wind.

Oliver! He was in there! Buried somewhere in that pile of rubbish.

'*Oliver, Oliver!*' Frantically she shouted his name over and over again. 'Oliver, where are you?'

A faint answering call led her to the very centre of the bricks and wood that had once been Shangri-La. She scrambled and crawled and dragged her way to him, crying helplessly, almost afraid of what she might find.

When she saw him, the lower half of his body weighted down by a heavy beam that must once have been part of the roof structure, so great was her relief that at least there were no visible signs of injury that she threw herself at him. 'Oh, Oliver, darling, my love, I was so afraid! You could have been killed!' She was kissing his cheeks, his eyes, his hair. 'Oh, my God, I don't think I could have stood it if I'd lost you as well as Shangri-La!'

His arms were about her too, holding her close. Their mouths met and clung, his predicament for the moment forgotten. He said at length, 'Darling Amie, you don't know what it's done to me to hear you say those words. I love you too. You've been tearing me apart by your apparent indifference. If you'd stayed here I was going to sell up and leave Mauritius for good. I couldn't have stood seeing you, loving you, but knowing that you preferred someone like Marcel.'

'Forget Marcel,' she said brusquely. 'We've got to get you out of here. Can you feel your legs— are they broken?'

He shook his head. 'I don't think so—numb, because of the length of time I've been here, and these beams are so damn heavy.'

'I must go for help,' she said, forcing herself to loose him and stand up. 'Where's the nearest place?'

'Don't be daft,' he returned. 'Everybody will be looking after themselves. It's up to you, you've got to move this thing somehow.'

'How can I?' asked Amie desperately. 'If you haven't the strength how do you expect me to be able to move it?'

'Between us we can,' he said compulsively, 'between us.'

She looked at him doubtfully.

'Get down on your knees,' he ordered. 'Now put your hands underneath, like this.'

For the first time she noticed Oliver's own hands, the nails torn and bleeding. 'Oh, Oliver!' she cried, her tears beginning all over again.

'I've been moving the bricks,' he said crisply.

'I thought I might be able to ease my legs out if I removed enough, but it didn't work. At least, though, it will enable us to get a hold of this damn timber.'

Amie inserted her left hand alongside his and pushed and heaved with all her might. 'It's no good,' she sobbed, 'I'm not strong enough, we'll just have to find someone else.'

'Use your other hand as well,' he barked tersely. 'I felt it move, it only needs a bit more pressure.'

'But I can't,' she cried, 'you know I can't.'

'Try,' he commanded. '*Amie, you've got to try. If you love me enough then do it for my sake. You're my only hope.*'

She was crying so much now that she couldn't even see what she was doing. Oliver guided her hands beneath the restricting rafter. 'Now lift,' he said, 'lift and push at the same time.'

Even before she tried she knew it was no use. 'I can't do it,' she wept, 'Oliver, I can't!'

'You can,' he insisted, teeth gritted, veins standing out on his face. 'You can, you must. *Amie, you must!*'

His impassioned plea somehow got through to her and desperation gave her strength. Miraculously she felt the wood against her fingers and she pushed with all her might, encouraged by Oliver at her side. 'Come on, Amie, you can do it, my darling, I know you can. Just a little bit more.'

Suddenly the beam moved and just as swiftly Oliver dragged himself free. Amie collapsed in a heap beside him. 'Oliver, I did it, I made my hand work! *You* made it better. Look——' She held her hand before his eyes, 'I can move my fingers! Oh,

Oliver, I love you, I love you!'

He was crying too, they were both crying and laughing at the same time, clinging, rolling over in the dirt, aware of nothing except their desperate need for each other.

It was a long time before they spoke again, and when they did Amie asked, 'What happened, Oliver? How did you manage to get stuck?'

'I was trying to see if I could salvage anything,' he said ruefully. 'It slipped and trapped me before I had time to get out of the way.'

'Thank God you aren't hurt,' she breathed fervently.

'And I thank God for giving you back the use of your hand.' He kissed the palm tenderly and then folded her fingers over it.

'He must have forgiven me,' she whispered, hardly realising that she had spoken aloud.

'For what, my darling?'

She looked at him with tear-filled eyes. 'For killing Ginny. It was God's way of punishing me, did you know? But now He must have decided I've taken enough. I'm sorry it was your sister. We didn't know. We thought she was an orphan.'

'There were just the two of us,' he said sadly. 'When our parents died Ginny was taken into a home, but I ran away to sea. I wanted none of that. We lost touch, although I've been trying to trace her for years. It was her dropping the Maxwell that did it.'

Amie frowned. 'What do you mean?'

'Virginia Maxwell-Jones, that was her proper name. It's funny, isn't it? I dropped the Jones and she the Maxwell. But there are more Joneses than there are Maxwells and I had a hell of a game tracing her—and when I did it was too late.'

'Do you blame me—for her death?' Amie's voice was hushed. She didn't think she could bear it if he did.

Oliver shook his head. 'No, my dearest.'

'Then why did you walk out of the flat when you found out it was me?'

He kissed her gently. 'I was upset. You can hardly blame me for that, can you? I was in no fit state to console you, so I thought it best I went. And I think it's time we went back to the bungalow. Poor Hobby will be thinking we're both hurt.'

They held hands and arrived laughing and happy, despite the chaos and turmoil all around them. The door was open and Amie suddenly realised what a sight they must look, their clothes torn, their bodies covered in dust and dirt and dried blood, streaks down their faces where they had cried.

Hobby took one look at them, at their happy smiling faces, and burst into tears herself. 'What's the matter?' asked Amie. 'We're safe, aren't you glad?'

'Of course I'm glad,' jerked Hobby, 'that's why I'm crying.'

'Then I'll tell you something that will make you happier still,' said Oliver, grinning. He held up Amie's hand. 'Wriggle your fingers,' he ordered, and Amie did.

Hobby's mouth fell open. 'It's a miracle!'

'And here's another miracle,' said Oliver. 'Amie and I are going to be married.'

Amie looked at him slyly. 'You haven't asked me yet—I might say no.'

'That's why I'm not asking you,' he returned darkly. 'I'm telling you. There's no way you're going to get out of it.'

Hobby was beside herself with joy, hugging first one and then the other. 'Congratulations,' she said, 'and about time too, if I might say so. Now I suggest you both go and get yourselves cleaned up while I make a nice cup of tea.'

'Tea?' threatened Oliver, picking her up by the waist and swinging her round. 'I think this calls for something stronger. There's a bottle of champagne in the cupboard, saved for a special occasion.'

Once they had showered and donned clean clothes Oliver opened the champagne. Hobby announced that she had never drunk champagne before, but reckoned she could quite acquire a taste for it if she had it often enough.

'I want to wish you both every happiness,' she continued, suddenly serious. 'I'd begun to think that you'd never come to your senses. As a matter of fact I was considering doing a bit of interfering. There's things you ought to know, Oliver, that Amie's never told you. If she had there'd have been none of this nonsense.'

'About Marcel?' he asked darkly.

Amie nodded, her laughter for the moment disappearing. 'I would have told you, eventually, but since Hobby's brought it up I suppose I may as well tell you now.'

'I think you had,' he said grimly.

He was thinking the worst, thought Amie, and smiled. 'Don't look so worried, Oliver, I've never fancied Marcel, not really, only that first day, and I've never been to bed with him, despite what you think.'

The relief on his face made her smile widen. 'It's quite a long story,' she went on. 'In fact it goes back to that night you had trouble at the factory. Marcel came, while you were away. I'd gone to bed because I was tired of waiting. When I heard someone in the room I thought it was you, and I'm afraid I invited you into bed with me.'

Oliver looked suitably surprised. 'That bit I like, but Marcel, he didn't——?'

'He tried,' she admitted sadly, 'and we had one hell of a struggle. I managed to run away—that was when I bumped my head. I think it saved me, because I knocked myself out and Marcel must have thought I was hiding because he gave up his search and disappeared.'

By the time she had finished Oliver was looking extremely angry. 'Why the hell didn't you tell me all this at the time?' he asked violently. 'I'd have killed him—I still will when I lay my hands on him.'

'No, Oliver.' She placed her hand on his arm—her right hand—and marvelled anew that the feeling had returned to her fingers. She could feel the fine springy hairs, the powerful muscles—it really was a miracle. 'It's all over now. Let's forget it. Once we're married he'll realise that he has absolutely no chance with me.'

Oliver's breathing was deep and erratic, his mouth grim. 'What I want to know is why you went out with him again after he'd tried to rape you?'

'He blackmailed me,' she said apologetically. 'He

threatened to ruin you if I didn't. You see, it was
he who tampered with your machines in the first
place, to get his own back on you for forbidding
me to go out with him.'

Oliver nodded. 'He'd already got it in for me
because he thought I'd once taken his girl. I hadn't,
but that's what he liked to think. But did you have
to stay out with him all night? Are you sure that
nothing——'

'I didn't stay out all night,' said Amie patiently.

'But I phoned, and there was no reply.'

'I know. I heard it ringing as I got back to the
house, but it stopped before I could get in and
answer it. I thought it might be you.'

'Marcel didn't go in with you?'

She shook her head. 'No way. As a matter of fact
I was so upset over the whole thing that I'd made
up my mind to come and tell you all about it the
next morning. But I was too late, you'd left.'

'I couldn't stop and see you making a fool of
yourself with Marcel,' he said tightly, 'not loving
you the way I did.'

'If you'd only told me!' Amie brushed her lips
gently across his cheek.

'When I thought you'd laugh?' he questioned
sadly. 'When I thought you'd fling my love back in
my face? I was afraid of making a fool of myself.
But I did phone you from London the next day.
You see, despite the fact that I'd gone away because
of you, I needed to keep in touch. Where were
you then?'

She pulled a rueful face. 'Barricading myself in
against Marcel. He was becoming a nuisance,
though I think since then he's realised there's no

hope. As a matter of fact we had a talk on the phone the other day. I told him we'd argued and I think he actually felt sorry for me. I got the feeling he was going to come and put things right between you, but I suppose the cyclone put a stop to that.'

'I reckon it's put a stop to a lot of things,' Oliver said grimly. 'I must see what the damage is at the factory. Do you mind if I go now? Will you two be all right if I disappear for an hour or two?'

'So long as you promise to be careful,' said Amie.

'I will, don't worry. My future has never been so rosy. I have no intention of doing anything to spoil it.'

They cooked a meal while he was away and discussed what Hobby would do once Amie and Oliver were married.

'I shall go back to London,' said Hobby firmly.

'No, you won't,' replied Amie severely. 'You'll stay and live with us. You can be our housekeeper. I don't suppose we shall stay here, it won't be big enough, especially once we start a family.' Her cheeks coloured delightfully at the thought. 'But I want you with me for always, Hobby.'

Mrs Hobbs looked inordinately pleased. 'You're a good girl, Amie. If I'd had a daughter I'd have wanted her to be just like you.'

When Oliver came back he looked grim.

'Is the factory all right?' asked Amie quickly.

'Oh, yes, no problem there, but the crops are flattened. I'm afraid we shall have a bad year.'

'Does it matter, my darling, so long as we have each other?' asked Amie, sliding her arms round his waist and pressing herself against him, relishing the feeling of warmth and security.

'If you don't mind being poor,' he mouthed against her ear, nibbling delicately and sending exquisite shivers through her body.

'With your love I'm the richest person in the world,' she said softly, adding after a pause, 'There are only two things that bother me.'

'And what are they, my sweetest? Nothing must worry my future wife, nothing at all.'

'First of all—Peta,' she began.

But even before she could voice her fears he said firmly, 'Peta means nothing to me, and there's nothing between us. It's all in her mind. Satisfied?'

Amie nodded selfconsciously.

'And what else is it that's bothering you, my sweet?'

She said hesitantly, 'I want to put it straight about Uncle Philippe. I'd never heard of him until I was told about my inheritance. Honestly, Oliver, I would have at least written to him if I'd known— my mother never told me she had a brother.'

'Then why the heck didn't you tell me that in the beginning?' he asked harshly, but he wasn't cross.

'Because I thought you'd think I was making it up so that you wouldn't think too badly of me.'

'You silly goose,' he laughed, 'but I must admit I am relieved. I didn't like the idea of my wife being mercenary.' He held her away from him. 'No more problems?'

She shook her head, brilliant green eyes resting on his face.

'Aren't you a little bit sad about Shangri-La?'

'I suppose so,' she said consideringly, 'but more

for my uncle's sake than my own. So long as I'm with you I don't care where we live.'

Oliver suddenly began to laugh, his whole body shaking with uncontrollable mirth.

'What's so funny?' she questioned huffily.

'Can't you see?' he choked. 'We both wanted Shangri-La, we've been fighting each other over it for the last goodness knows how many months, and now neither of us have it.'

Amie joined in his laughter. 'Why were you so against me turning it into a hotel?'

'Because, my darling, I planned to make it our home, once we were married.'

'But you didn't even know I loved you.'

'It was what your uncle wanted,' he said confidently, 'and I had no intention of letting him down. We'll build another house on the same spot, we'll even call it Shangri-La, if you like.'

'Can we afford it?' she asked. 'Especially if you're going to have a bad year with the sugar.'

Oliver gave a secretive smile. 'You didn't really think I'd let that insurance lapse, did you? Not when I knew without a shadow of doubt that Shangri-La would be my home one day.'

His confidence irked and Amie lashed out, but she didn't mean it, and when he gathered her close, she lifted her face readily for his kiss. Hobby looked at them serenely and smiled, knowing that for the next few minutes her presence would be totally forgotten.

The Mills & Boon Rose is the Rose of Romance

Every month there are ten new titles to choose from — ten new stories about people falling in love, people you want to read about, people in exciting, far-away places. Choose Mills & Boon. It's your way of relaxing:

March's titles are:

GREGG BARRATT'S WOMAN by *Lilian Peake*
Why was that disagreeable Gregg Barratt so sure that what had happened to Cassandra was her sister Tanis's fault?

FLOODTIDE by *Kay Thorpe*
A stormy relationship rapidly grew between Dale Ryland and Jos Blakeman. What had Jos to give anyone but bitterness and distrust?

SAY HELLO TO YESTERDAY by *Sally Wentworth*
It had to be coincidence that Holly's husband Nick — whom she had not seen for seven years — was on this remote Greek island? Or was it?

BEYOND CONTROL by *Flora Kidd*
Kate was in love with her husband Sean Kierly, but what was the point of clinging to a man who so obviously didn't love her?

RETRIBUTION by *Charlotte Lamb*
Why had the sophisticated Simon Hilliard transferred his attentions from Laura's sister to Laura herself, who wasn't as capable as her sister of looking after herself?

A SECRET SORROW by *Karen van der Zee*
Could Faye Sherwood be sure that Kai Ellington's love would stand the test if and when she told him her tragic secret?

MASTER OF MAHIA by *Gloria Bevan*
Lee's problem was to get away from New Zealand and the dour Drew Hamilton. Or *was* that her real problem?

TUG OF WAR by *Sue Peters*
To Dee Lawrence's dismay and fury every time she met Nat Archer, he always got the better of her. Why didn't he just go away?

CAPTIVITY by *Margaret Pargeter*
Chase Marshall had offered marriage to Alex, simply because he thought she was suitable. Well, he could keep his offer!

TORMENTED LOVE by *Margaret Mayo*
Amie's uncle had hoped she would marry his heir Oliver Maxwell. But how could she marry a maddening man like that?

The Mills & Boon Rose is the Rose of Romance

Every month there are ten new titles to choose from — ten new stories about people falling in love, people you want to read about, people in exciting, far-away places. Choose Mills & Boon. It's your way of relaxing:

April's titles are:

THE STORM EAGLE *by Lucy Gillen*
In other circumstances Chiara would have married Campbell Roberts. But he had not consulted her. And now wild horses wouldn't make her accept him!

SECOND-BEST BRIDE *by Margaret Rome*
Angie would never have guessed how the tragedy that had befallen Terzan Helios would affect her own life ...

WOLF AT THE DOOR *by Victoria Gordon*
Someone had to win the battle of wills betwwen Kelly Barnes and her boss Grey Scofield, in their Rocky Mountains camp ...

THE LIGHT WITHIN *by Yvonne Whittal*
Now that Roxy might recover her sight, the misunderstanding between her and Marcus Fleming seemed too great for anything to bridge it ...

SHADOW DANCE *by Margaret Way*
If only her new job assignment had helped Alix to sort out the troubled situation between herself and her boss Carl Danning!

SO LONG A WINTER *by Jane Donnelly*
'You'll always be too young and I'll always be too old,' Matt Hanlon had told Angela five years ago. Was the situation any different now?

NOT ONCE BUT TWICE *by Betty Neels*
Christina had fallen in love at first sight with Professor Adam ter Brandt. But hadn't she overestimated his interest in her?

MASTER OF SHADOWS *by Susanna Firth*
The drama critic Max Anderson had wrecked Vanessa's acting career with one vicious notice, and then Vanessa became his secretary ...

THE TRAVELLING KIND *by Janet Dailey*
Charley Collins knew that she must not get emotionally involved with Shad Russell. But that was easier said than done ...

ZULU MOON *by Gwen Westwood*
In order to recover from a traumatic experience Julie went to Zululand, and once again fell in love with a man who was committed elsewhere ...

If you have difficulty in obtaining any of these books from your local paperback retailer, write to:

Mills & Boon Reader Service
P.O. Box 236, Thornton Road, Croydon, Surrey, CR9 3RU.

Masquerade
Historical Romances

Intrigue
excitement
romance

CHANGE OF HEART
by Margaret Eastvale

Edmund, Lord Ashorne, returned from the Peninsular Wars to find that his fiancée had married his cousin. It was her sister Anne who had remained single for his sake!

LION OF LANGUEDOC
by Margaret Pemberton

Accused of witchcraft by Louis XIV's fanatical Inquisitor, Marietta was rescued by Léon de Villeneuve — the Lion of Languedoc. How could she *not* fall in love with him, even knowing that he loved another woman?

Look out for these titles in your local paperback shop from 13th March 1981